# HAWECHA

## A WOMAN FOR ALL TIME

BY

RHODIA MANN

Published by **Sasa Sema** Publications
*An imprint of Longhorn Publishers*

Longhorn Publishers (U) Ltd.,
Plot M220, Ntinda Industrial Area.,
Jinja Road, P.O. Box 24745,
Kampala, Uganda.

Longhorn Publishers (K) Ltd.,
Funzi Road, Industrial Area,
P.O. Box 18033-00500,
Nairobi, Kenya.

Longhorn Publishers (T) Ltd.,
Msasani Village, Block F, House No. 664,
Old Bagamoyo Road,
Dar es Salaam, Tanzania.



First published 2008

Cover design by Longhorn Publishers

**ISBN 9966 951 44-X**

Printed by Printpoint Ltd, Changamwe Road,
Industrial Area, P.O. Box 30975,
Nairobi, Kenya.

# FOREWORD

The Oromo people are Eastern Cushitic, a sub-group of the Galla. They were pushed southwards by the Somalis — perhaps as long ago as the tenth century. After several hundred years, they migrated even further south into the southern part of what is now Ethiopia.

Sometime around the middle of the sixteenth century, another sub-group of the Galla — called Borana — occupied land originally inhabited by the Oromo. Gradually, the Borana moved further and further southwards into what is today known as Kenya.

In Ethiopia, there are perhaps 23 million Oromo — making them one of the most numerous peoples in Africa. The Borana living in Kenya number roughly 80,000. The separation is mainly one of national boundaries. Both the Borana and the Oromo share the same customs, and a common political legal system. They also share the same spiritual beliefs and the same spiritual leadership.

The history of the people — who claim to be over 3,000 years old — is handed down via oral historians, who inherit this role from their fathers or other close relatives.

In 1987, I met one of the oral historians of the tribe who was also regarded as a ritual expert and spiritual leader. His name is Dabassah Guyo Saffaro. Dabassah was born in southern Ethiopia.

When Mengistu came into power (1974) and began his reign of Red Terror, communism was the only religion tolerated. Wishing to uphold his traditional beliefs, Dabassah chose exile. He migrated southwards into Kenya, eventually reaching the outskirts of Nairobi, Kenya's capital. He said he had been guided there by the star Sirius, the most important star in Oromo tradition.

By the time of our meeting, Dabassah had created a traditional sacred site near Nairobi for Borana people who had moved to that area. Furthermore, he was giving regular Borana language religious broadcasts over the Kenya radio.

A friendship arose between us, and before long he became my teacher. In time, I acquired some knowledge of cosmology, stars, legends, numerology, divination techniques and animal totems. I also learned of spirit guides and teachers.

The friendship deepened. I was made welcome at prayers and ceremonies, asked to organise my own, and given an Oromo name. Eventually, I was invited to create a new sacred site for Dabassah's people.

In all the great wealth of cultural information I received over the years, one legend stands out as being quite remarkable. It is the story of a simple Oromo woman who gradually arose to a position of spiritual prominence, as a healer and prophetess and became a part of oral history. In a male-dominated society, this was a remarkable achievement. Her story is the inspiration for this book.

According to tradition, Hawecha died roughly two hundred years ago. Visits to Boranaland as well as invitations to month-long major ceremonies held on the Kenya/Ethiopia border in 1995 gave me the necessary visual and cultural framework to her life. This was enhanced by visits to both the Ethnography Department of the National Museum of Kenya and the Ethnographic Museum in Addis Ababa. I also journeyed by car southwards from there into the region Hawecha is said to have lived in.

An assortment of books and papers (some unpublished) and several visits to the Library of the British Institute in Eastern Africa (based in Nairobi), yielded further information.

Discussions with Dabassah and other elders filled in a few more gaps.

Dabassah gave me only the briefest account of Hawecha's life, including her death and what she foretold beyond it. I have 'embroidered' upon his outline — turning a short story into a 'historical novel'. Hawecha has become the vehicle for me to offer glimpses into a fascinating and little-known culture.

When I attended the ceremonies in 1995, I was told these differed little from those of the Oromo forebears. This may well be so, since the Oromo/Borana pride themselves on adhering to tradition to a remarkable degree. I recorded what I could ... and then allowed for a more "primitive" epoch — one without cloth, aluminium and other modernities.

I at last felt able to put Hawecha into the appropriate historical, social and cultural context.

Whether to use vernacular words became a major issue. For the sake of simplicity, I decided to leave most of these out, using only those I consider most important. As to my choice of Oromifta spelling, having read many learned variations, I have again opted for simplicity and kept mine largely phonetic.

I tried to imagine what life must have been like over two hundred years ago in Hawecha's birthplace. Not having any literature to fall back on, I have had to — in a sense — invent. Ultimately, I feel as though the story "wrote itself"!

In the small town of Sololo, just south of the Ethiopian border, there is a Catholic mission established by the Comboni missionaries. The duties of the mission include providing a modern education for the Borana people who live around them.

It was not difficult to find boys to educate, but when it came to the schooling of young girls, the fathers were adamant. "Boys are like the sun, but girls are like the moon." Not one was willing to send his daughter to school.

The turning point came in 1986, through the brilliant idea of one of the Catholic Fathers. He studied Oromo/Borana culture in depth to find a source of inspiration. He came upon the legend of Hawecha. What better role model could he want?

He founded the Hawecha Girls Primary School. Then, he made the rounds of the fathers. "I will give a free education to your son, if you will also give me your daughter!" Perseverance paid off and the school opened with twelve young girls registered as pupils.

In 1994, the first Borana girl attended the University of Nairobi, Kenya's capital. By 1995, there were 200 girls at the Hawecha Girls' Primary School. In 1998, three girls were offered places in a Nairobi commercial college. The story continues ....

A woman who died two hundred years ago was the cause of all this. The Hawecha legend lives on!

Rhodia Mann
Nairobi, Kenya.

September 2006.

# PROLOGUE

The old woman sat hunched over the embers of her small fire. The hut stank. Nobody had swept it today. She stirred the ashes idly with her foot: a foot once small and dainty, now grown thick-soled and broad, with the little toe splayed outwards. A foot good for walking many miles. She sighed. Ah, the miles those feet of hers had walked! North and south. To the rising sun, to the western hills . . . and even round in circles.

She was tired now. Her life stretched long and far behind her. A useful life, she felt.

Now, that life was nearing its completion; she had had her dream. One of those momentous dreams that interspersed the months and years of her life — a dream of undeniable power. It had troubled her greatly, until she had understood it fully. She was not afraid now. The dream had explained itself very beautifully.

That was why she sat here now, with the fire dying and growing cold. Cold, and old. Like her.

"Time to die," she thought. "You have outlived your usefulness, as well as all those whom you once loved. Ah yes! The stars have spoken and so has Suleh. It is time to go now."

A tear coursed down her old and raddled cheek. Once, she had been considered beautiful. Now, she was only old. Old and rather ugly.

The fire glowed softly, oh so softly, reminding her of her soul. "That is not old," she reminded herself. "By now, my soul is all I have. May God look after my soul, then, for I no longer can."

The old woman hobbled to her pile of goatskins, lay down and turned away from the fire towards the wall of the hut. She curled herself up into a tight little ball. And waited quietly for death.

# CHAPTER 1

Hawecha sat beneath the tall tree beside the river, brooding. It was a long time since she had seen her mother smile. What could a seven-year old do? Not much, it seemed. Hawecha sighed deeply.

Her father had died long ago. He had been stern, tall and proud; of the Gono half of the tribe. That meant that when she married, she would have to choose somebody from the Sabba half. That was the rule. Her father had drilled it into her. He had been a clan leader. Perhaps that was why he had to be so serious. Not easy to talk to. He hardly ever smiled. Why then did her mother miss him so?

Her mother was a beautiful woman even when her face was crinkled with lines of grief and worry. When Hawecha was little her mother had smiled a great deal, radiating joy around her. Then Dhaki had died. Hawecha had lost her pretty baby sister who cooed and gurgled at everyone.

Why? Hawecha wondered. Why did everybody have to die? Her small shoulders heaved as the tears streaked down her dusty cheeks.

Hawecha was a pensive, quiet child, introverted and usually lost in a world of her own. 'Hawecha-the-Dreamer', they called her in the village. Her mother was always admonishing her. "Come, girl! Be brighter now. It doesn't suit you to be in the moon and the stars. Put your feet on the ground and help me with the water!" Or: "Hawecha! Really! Watch where you put your feet. You'll burn them in the fire!"

Hawecha sighed again. She put her small feet on the ground, heaved herself up, and set off to help her mother. Water. Always the battle was for water. Dreams or not, they had to drink, to wash and visitors had to have their thirst quenched.

She trotted off towards her home: a round hut with a high roof, all made of woven branches. High and light and cool. There were sixteen huts in the village — all identical. Well, one was a little higher than the others. It belonged to Gababa Halakhe, their spiritual leader. His responsibilities were enormous. Perhaps he needed more shade in which to think all his important thoughts? His head must have been awfully full of thoughts.

The huts were arranged in something resembling a circle, with a vacant area in the centre where people gathered occasionally to dance or sing ... or just chat with each other if they had time. Three old trees grew there. The village had grown up around them.

To one side of the enclosure lived Buleh, their ritual leader. He was old now and a little forgetful. Out of respect, the villagers still referred to him in ceremonial matters, waiting patiently for him to make his ponderous decisions.

To protect the settlement from lions and hyenas, thick branches of thornbush had been piled up together to form a dense hedge around it. Each family had its own gateway. At night, thorny branches were pulled across these. Inside, all could sleep in peace and safety. Within the enclosure, each family had its own small corrals in which were kept all the livestock.

The Oromo were cattle rearing people, and loved their cattle almost as much as they loved their children. They worked hard to keep the cattle in good health, taking them to water daily and out to good pastures. The men talked to them to keep them contented. The women always sang to the cows, to make the milk happy.

Some of the families had goats, which had to be led out each day to browse upon the lower branches of the bushes. Every family had at least one donkey, whose job it was to carry heavy loads from here to there. They usually complained with loud hee-hawing and braying.

A short distance away from the village to the west stood an unusually large and shady tree. It was their place of prayer. Hawecha had only been there twice. She remembered the feel of the rough bark beneath her small hands and how the tree had towered above her, reaching up and up ... high up to the very skies. She had fallen asleep the first time. "Too young," her mother had supposed. The second time she had been alert and had followed the clapping and the singing. The words had been simple ones, with Gababa Halakhe leading them. All they had to do was form a loud chorus.

Her thoughts wandered to the people with whom she shared her life. Some were very strange like Hororo-The-Hairless-One, who had been born entirely bald, or Head-in-the-Stars, who had gone mad three years before. There was the young man who had been born with one leg all pulled up and bent beneath him. You could hardly call it a proper leg. Although he had been given three good names at his birth, all reminiscent of his lineage, he was commonly known as One-Leg.

Rufo-The-Chatterbox drove everybody crazy with her endless comments, musings and mental meanderings and Zugura-The-Storyteller often got completely lost in her own stories, never finding an ending.

The saddest person in the whole community was Tummeh-With-No-Nose. Her nose had been slowly eaten away by leprosy. Nobody had seen it, but everyone knew about it. Now she walked about with a goatskin pulled low over her forehead to hide the hideous gap beneath.

Hawecha felt sorry for her and would often stand next to her and simply stroke Tummeh's arm in silent compassion. Sometimes, the arm would reach out from beneath the goatskin and pull Hawecha closer. Strange snuffles would ensue. Hawecha knew the poor woman was weeping. Dignity demanded that she say nothing about it. All she could do was allow herself to be hugged.

As she followed the narrow path, kicking up dust as she walked, Hawecha thought of this great land of theirs that spread out far beyond them all.

Gababa Halakhe had spoken often and at length about the Oromo people. A proud race, of ancient lineage: "from further north," he had said. Now, they lived in Liban — right here. Hawecha was pleased with herself. She remembered things so well.

Once upon a time, oh so very long ago, the Oromo people had lived in a land called Fugug. Yes, she remembered being told that too. Then something bad had happened and all the Oromo had run away in many directions at once. Oh dear, she had forgotten what had happened to her ancestors. Something very, very bad!

Now they lived all over the world: in Oda, Tuqqa and Mega. Hawecha had never moved from this village. Those magical names were her only understanding of 'far.' One day, she would travel to Oda, Tuqqa and

Mega. Of this she had no doubt. Her spirits lifted as she thought of travelling. When she was all grown up and married, perhaps then, she would see the world.

"Mother, I'm here!" she cried, as she entered her mother's doorway. "Good, I had almost given up on you, girl! Put the water .... The water, girl! Did you forget to fill the water-pot for me? Useless child! Dear God, what am I to do with her? Widowed and one child gone. Can you make this one a better child for me?" Poor Ula moaned and groaned. Life was too hard for play.

Hawecha hung her head in shame. She had filled her head up with Fugug and Tuqqa and now her mother's heart had broken. "Don't break, mother dear. Please don't break for me!" She flung her little arms about her mother's thin shoulders. "I'll go back again. It isn't far, and I like the river. I'll go back, don't worry. And I haven't lost your water-pot. I remember just where I put it down."

Twirling round — all large eyes and seriousness — Hawecha retraced her steps. As she followed her own footprints, her attention wandered yet again. 'Head-in-the-Clouds' had taken over. She began to think of Sirius, the star that guided her people. Old Hababa Galakhe had told the children all about Sirius. How the star brought them closer to God ... if they listened and obeyed . . . and how very important it was to listen. Thoughts of Sirius took her to the Milky Way and all the myriad stars that were supposed to speak to them at night. She had never spoken to a star. Perhaps one day she would.

The water-pot lay where she had left it, propped against the fattest root of the tree. She picked it up carefully and struggled with it down to the river bank. The river gurgled as she lowered the pot into its ripples. Half full and then she hauled it out. Half full. That was all she could manage. She then raised it carefully to her head, as all women do. Slowly, with a straight back, she walked all the way to her home.

Darmi was there. Hawecha lowered the water-pot and placed it on the ground near the three stones of the hearth. She liked Darmi. Her mother always brightened up when Darmi came to visit. The two ladies chatted about the men-folk, about the kinsfolk and about the newest baby. They talked of illnesses, herbs and 'women's problems'. Oh, they chatted on and on! Hawecha smiled. Her mother had so few friends. How good it was to see her smile and hear her laugh.

At last Darmi left to feed the baby. Dusk had settled upon the village: a warm and saffron glow. The water boiled. The meal was cooked. And still her mother smiled.

The stars came out and Hawecha turned over in her bed. It was made of branches lashed together. Over it, three goatskins were laid. She snuggled down for the night, thinking how good life was. All her thoughts were warm ones. She smiled and kissed the stars goodnight.

# CHAPTER 2

The next day was a day of prayers for the mothers of the tribe. Dutifully, Hawecha accompanied hers to the holy tree. A circle had been cleared around it. The sacred place had five entrances in honour of the five High Priests of the Oromo people. They entered through the eastern opening and sat down at the base of the tree, waiting for old Gababa Halakhe to speak.

"Today, I will tell you of Suleh, a woman high in the ranks of women. She lived long ago, in Fugug, and still helps those who need her. She is wise and knows us all. If you look up at the Milky Way at night, those stars are her companions.

Hawecha wriggled excitedly, nudging her friend Choleh to make sure she too was equally excited.

The teacher adjusted his goatskins, and sat down in front of them all, planting his white stick in the ground before him. Everybody sat still now. All the teachers had to tell good stories. Hawecha's eyes opened wide, to absorb every single word.

"Suleh grew up in our Fatherland, quite far from where we are now," the sage began. "She lived with her parents and was a good child .... as all small girls should be." His eyes blazed fire as he looked around at the six or seven daughters gathered there. "And small boys too," he admonished, to make sure they too were listening attentively.

"Suleh grew into a beautiful woman and the time came for her to marry. Her parents had chosen a young man for her, from the Karayyu clan. All the bridal gifts had been given. All was ready for the ceremony.

One night, Suleh had a dream, in which she saw a great lion. It pounced on her and tried to eat her up. She understood at once that this was what her marriage would do to her. She would lose her soul. She told her parents of her dream, but they would not listen. Unthinkable for a daughter not to marry. She cried a whole puddle of tears, just trying to make them listen.

Suleh called upon God to help her. She prayed and prayed and prayed for help, so that her soul would survive. She stopped eating and moped about the hut, refusing to emerge. She turned thin and weepy.

According to the laws of the tribe, every woman should marry. In despair, her parents consulted a diviner. He was a thrower-of-sandals. Flap, flap! The sandals fell far apart. 'Not good. Flap! The left one covered the right. 'Not good at all. The girl might die from grief.' He threw them yet again. 'Death, death, pain!' In the end, he convinced her parents that marriage was useless for Suleh. What destiny then lay ahead for her? They asked the old man to throw again.

Frowning in concentration, he spat on the left sandal, and then on the right one, tossed them in the air and studied the pattern they made upon the ground and in his mystical mind. At long last, he emerged from his personal vision, and spoke. "This one will be a teacher. This one has much to learn. Nobody can teach her. She must learn all by herself."

Gababa Halakhe raised his head and studied the children in front of him. They sat upright, their eyes alert with interest. He had captured their hearts and souls with his story. All was as it should be.

"This is the law of our people. If one child is chosen for a higher purpose, then that child must be helped. It is a long, slow road. The legend does not tell us how long it took Suleh to learn. All we know is that she sits with God as one of his High Councillors. She is a wonderful soul. I have seen her twice. She is good, kind, and helpful. She is an example of perfect womanhood. That is why all the Oromo love her."

Long after the prayers for the mothers of the tribe were finished, long after the children had run around the tree singing and clapping their hands, Hawecha felt the presence of Suleh near her.

That night, she tossed and turned and moaned aloud in her sleep. She trod upon a star and did not know which one it was. Then she saw another star, turning over and over. Blue, it was; shining dim, then bright, then dim again, repeatedly.

Suddenly, she saw the face of a young woman, brown like herself, with smooth, unwrinkled skin. The woman smiled at her in such a kind and sweet way. "I am Suleh, Hawecha. I have come to talk to you. You need to sleep now. I will look after you for as long as you live. Sleep now, little one: sleep."

Hawecha gave a great sigh and rolled over onto her stomach, then onto her back again. She relaxed. Her head emptied completely. The troublesome stars moved away and a gentle breeze blew about her head. She felt carefree, warm and loved. At last, she fell into dreamless sleep.

In the morning, she spoke of her dream to her mother, who was more than a little worried. Her mother, Ayo Midadu — the Beautiful Lady — had also been a Dreamer. It had brought her fame but not much happiness. Ula wanted a normal life for her daughter: a husband and many children. "Great God, I don't know what to do," she thought. "I want a normal life for her. I hope she is not being chosen."

Days became weeks and the weeks turned into months and years. The seasons changed over and over. Time passed and Hawecha seemed quite happy. Ula felt her prayers had been answered. She watched Hawecha play with Choleh in between the household tasks. "At last! She is outgrowing that dreadful phase."

One day, all the girls who had reached puberty were called together for a special ceremony just for them. There were only six girls who qualified: Hawecha stood amongst them.

Three old women led them outside the compound and across the savannah. They were heading for an ancient tree, long used as a sacred site. The girls followed their leaders in silence, as was the custom. It would be a long walk.

When they arrived, Hawecha saw that the tree was low-built, with many spiky branches: not the kind of tree you would associate with holiness. Not high and mighty, leading up to the heavens. Instead, it was a sheltering sort of tree.

From its lower branches hung small gifts that people had left there: strings of clay beads and twists of dried leaves containing tobacco. A bone had been wedged in between two small branches. Two small black leather pouches had been tied to branches higher up.

The girls were drawn close together and instructed to close their eyes. The eldest of the three women who had proved her great value to the tribe by producing seven sons in succession, and then a daughter who now stood there, began a chant in a low sing-song voice.

*"Father of us all, make these girls grow wise.*
*Make them wiser than their mothers.*
*Give them blessings in the form of children.*
*Teach them manners. Make them merciful.*
*This is the prayer, oh Wisest One!"*

The girls were stripped naked and their bodies smeared all over with cow fat. This had been brought in a small wooden container. It was rubbed well in, so that their limbs shone.

Old Dabbo, known as The-Mother-of-Many, then told each girl to smear some of the leftover fat onto the tree, as a sign that they had been there. Hawecha rubbed the fat near to where the small bone had been wedged. It seemed 'her' special place.

They left, feeling terribly important and mature. Now, they had left childhood behind them properly. Now, they could grow up. They sang as they walked along.

# CHAPTER 3

Shortly after this event, the village was thrown into shock. Gababa Halakhe died peacefully in his sleep. His body was taken out of the village, and wrapped in goatskins. Every single inhabitant laid aside whatever work was in progress in order to participate in the funeral.

The men chose an open area near to the place of prayer and dug a shallow grave there. They would have buried him beneath his beloved holy tree, had custom not prevented this.

The body was laid in its grave and each person threw in a few seeds, or a leaf, or a twig. Something growing, it had to be. Then they covered his remains with earth.

To mark the spot, they searched far and wide for large white stones, which they piled in a heap over his grave. The women wailed day and night. The elders prayed beside the grave for his soul to find peace. He had taught several generations of children: everybody felt his absence deeply. Who would advise them now? It was as though the world had ended.

Hawecha mourned harder than most and soon grew listless. She had adored him and it seemed he had seen something inside her that nobody else had noticed. He had often spoken to her alone, reminding her of ancestors and legends, of times long gone, of Fugug, of giants and of stars. His death cut deep into her heart. She would never be the same.

Suleh often visited her at night now, appearing in her dreams. "I will look after you. Have no fear." "Don't worry too much. I am here," and words of a similar nature. Once, Suleh appeared through a great, dark cloud, as if she had parted it and brought in the sunshine.

Hawecha loved her nights. No matter what troubled her during the daytime, her sleep always brought her sweet visions. Her sorrows were far from over, however.

One day, as Ula was walking back from the river with water, she felt a great pain in her chest — a stab that went right through her. She sat down suddenly in the path and tried to catch her breath. Another stab, in her back this time. She lay down on the path, frozen in fear and panic. Her head spun faster and faster. The water spilled out from her water-pot. It seeped into the ground

The women found her there, asleep forever. They carried her frail body into her hut and gathered around to weep. She was laid to rest beyond the village — not near Gababa Halakhe — but towards the rising sun.

Ula had always loved the sunrise. Three black stones were placed at her head to mark the place. They told the whole world that a good woman lay there: the mortal remains of the one-who-had-been. The soul already lived on elsewhere.

Hawecha stood there in a stupor. Had she been older, she would have remained in her parents' hut. Being still too young for this, custom dictated that it be vacated immediately. Her material needs were taken care of at once by her mother's sister, a kindly woman named Galgalu.

"We will take care of you, your uncle Jarso and I. We would love to have another girl to live with us." She gave Hawecha a hug and wiped away the tears.

Jarso was a man who commanded great respect. Over the years, he had proved himself wise and careful in his choice of words. The High Priests had appointed him a senior councillor. His role required him to attend important meetings during which clan matters were discussed. From time to time, he was also invited elsewhere to larger gatherings concerning the welfare of the entire tribe.

There were two children in the home, both daughters, and both somewhat older than Hawecha. The elder of the two was called Wareh, a quiet, soft-spoken child. The younger one had been named Chuquliss, after her maternal grandmother. Like her namesake, Chuquliss was kind and gentle.

The women helped to clean out Ula's hut. They wrapped up her possessions and moved them into Galgalu's hut. "This is your inheritance," her aunt explained. "When you marry, you will need it all. Meanwhile, it is safe with me."

Ula's hut was burned down to the ground. It was not good for anyone else to occupy it. As the flames rose higher and higher about her past, Hawecha sobbed her heart out.

"This girl needs a great deal of love." Galgalu had told her daughters. They gave their best, but ... being older ... they were often pressed for time.

Hawecha settled in as best as she could, determined to please her new family.

# CHAPTER 4

As if in answer to Hawecha's need for joy and adventure, a long line of horses plodded into the village one day, clearly exhausted from the long journey they had made. "From Aksum," the leader of the caravan explained ... "a journey of many moons from here."

He was a swarthy man, somewhat scrofulous in appearance. He had only one tooth in his mouth. Hawecha could not take her eyes off him. It seemed he had not been near water in many weeks. He reeked of sweat and urine as if he had never enough time in which to relieve himself completely. Hawecha wrinkled up her small nose in disgust.

Much taken with his clothing, she studied this in detail. He wore not skins as her folk did, but something which she learned was called 'calico' — cotton which came from India, a large land ... large, like theirs.

Timidly, Hawecha approached to feel this new substance, soiled and stained though it was. The leader was a natural braggart, all too eager to show off. He lifted up his long and dirty shirt, to show her the baggy trousers beneath, tied at the waist with a leather thong. Hawecha stretched out her hand to touch the fabric gently. "It bends well," was her admiring comment. The two other men in the caravan wore similar attire.

The star in the "Caravan of New Delights" was a young woman — the leader's sister. She wore long skirts of something bright red that swished as she walked by. She invited Hawecha to touch it. Soft, pliant and shot with threads of gold. Luxurious, intimidating ... captivating! Nazrah told Hawecha that what she wore was called silk — only for the richest of women. Hawecha noticed a small tear at the hem and three brown stains down the front. A slattern: the worst kind of woman in the world, according to tradition. Laughingly, Nazrah moved away to attend to business.

Hawecha turned her attention to the horses that formed the caravan. She listened to the fire they breathed and watched the heaving of their sweaty flanks. Their eyes were enormous — the largest she had ever seen. Terrified, she skulked behind the other women, peering out every now and then with unbearable curiosity. The horses pawed the ground in anger, she assumed, and snorted as if anxious to depart.

From their backs, great packs were taken down and the goods displayed for barter in the very centre of the village. "I trade for goatskins or for grain," the leader announced.

Two horses were laden with packets of salt, tied up neatly in dried banana leaves. She knew all about salt, and turned away in disdain, as one or two packets were opened. 'Is this all they bring us?' she wondered. "What a useless journey to bring us what we already know and have!"

Galgalu bartered for two packets, yet she had one stored neatly in her home. "I need much, much more than you think," she explained. "And I don't know when the next chance will come."

As the remaining packs were opened, Hawecha's eyes opened wide with wonder. Such goods, such riches, such surprises!

The third horse had been laden with clay pots of different sizes. One was for water, large and stout. Another was for milk, another for special occasions when one had to impress one's guests. It had a graceful spout, and a beautifully shaped handle. A fourth was for 'in between' as the clever trader had explained, persuading each and every housewife that only a complete set of four was worth buying.

"Up north, the women do not consider themselves proper women without these four dignified pots, lined up against the wall."

Soon, not a single clay pot remained. The bartering had been garrulous and heated. The women of her village had lost almost all their dignity in haggling over these.

The fourth horse carried small packets of spices. Hawecha's nostrils flared at each new fragrance. Her aunt had never cooked with spices. Nor had any of her friends. These were new commodities. Hawecha listened hard to learn the new names. Foreign names. Exciting ones!

"Now this is cardamom," the young woman explained as she untied a small packet to reveal its contents. The seeds were small, oval and light brown, contained in a whitish husk. The air was filled with the new aroma. "This will help your married life!" She announced, raising her eyebrows, so that the villagers knew precisely to what she alluded. Her smile was full of innuendo. They understood her. Within moments, not a single packet of cardamom was left.

Next, the wily saleswoman opened up a packet of chilli peppers. "From India. From the land where one of your forebears lived." Cleverly, she wove in a little history. "We have heard of her, a lovely lady . . . and she cooked miracles up for her man. A little bit of this and a pinch of that. And, lo and behold ... her husband adored her!"

Before long, the chilli had disappeared also.

Next came cumin. "Good for the stomach!" the Somali girl shouted. "Very good for flatulence. Helps you sleep well at night in the sweet and clean air." The seeds lay small and thin in the palm of her hand. Again, not a packet was left.

"And now, I show you cloves, which come from a different land." A strong and pungent smell assailed them. "The land is surrounded by water, which reaches to the very ends of the world. God put it there to astound us. It has a beautiful name." The women all leaned forwards to hear it.

"It is called Zanzibar — a place of blessed breezes, coolness and fresh ideas. Ah, Allah designed it well!" She enchanted them with descriptions of its fine sandy beaches, groves of clove trees ... and mangoes. "Alas, we could not bring you the fruit of God's own tree. It is too far. They would rot before you ate them."

She described the sweetness of the yellow fruit, the juiciness, the 'nectar of the gods' contained therein. Hawecha salivated at her words.

Needless to say, the cloves disappeared in a flash even though no woman in Hawecha's village had ever cooked with spices. "Fresh tastes make fresh minds," her aunt announced, nodding sagely. "I will keep them until the next festival — whatever it is. The spices are bound to come in useful."

From the fifth horse, a tired old mare beyond the capacity to bear anything heavier, were off-loaded neatly rolled-up mats. These were woven of *doum palm* fibres. The man in charge unfurled them upon the ground and immediately threw himself down upon one. "Ah, bliss," he pronounced, as he lay there, in a semblance of ecstasy. "Surely your neighbours, the *warr dasse* people, are past masters of the art of sleeping deeply. These mats are made in Heaven ... or at least under Allah's instructions."

Hawecha tugged at her aunt's skirts. Galgalu was rapt in the wonderland that the mats foretold. "Aunt!" Galgalu was far away, in some fool's paradise. "Aunt!" Hawecha twitched the skirts more forcibly. Finally, Galgalu paid attention.

"What's an Allah? Is it a horse?"

Galgalu smiled. "No dear, it's a kind of God — but not nearly as strong as ours! Ours rules the world. Ancient sages have said so."

The women returned to their homes to put their new (and expensive) acquisitions neatly away. Business was by no means finished, however.

The sixth horse was laden with goods for the menfolk only. Hawecha crept near to view these. The Somali trader unwrapped a long thin package of banana leaves and removed his sales item carefully from it. He waved it aloft and expounded upon its virtues.

"Here is an arrow the likes of which you have never seen!" he began. "Sharp, and with deadly poison at its tip. This is the work of a tribe your ancestors knew, called Ndorobo. Clever men they are, living from the land and all its fruits. They know every tree and bush. They move about with stealth, with special secret gifts Allah gave them. They are poor in land and own no livestock . . . yet they inhabit a vast territory and exploit its hidden riches thoroughly."

There were a dozen or so warriors in the village at the time and each one coveted these arrows, with their clever barbs and beautiful feathers, to ensure far and accurate flight. More than anything, however, they prized the poison at the tips. Bows were there, too, to make the flight of the arrows perfect. These were half the height of a man in length and great strength was required to bend them.

"The bows are from the Akamba people. They are such great hunters. Allah favours them in this. Their skills are world renowned."

Within minutes, eighty-two arrows had been purchased — each made by a great hunter of those fabled Ndorobo. And not one of the seventeen Akamba bows was left.

Also gone in a flash were twenty great round shields made of buffalo-hide, from the Aksumites, known far and wide for their prowess in battle. These were borne by the seventh horse, who stood prouder and taller than the others, as if conscious of the might of his burden.

"Although we are peaceful people, we must live with war in our hearts," Harero-the-Warrior commented. "In years to come, we will surely need all these. We are beset by enemies. New ones may rise against us. It is well to be prepared. Already the Turkana want our livestock. I will stock up now." The village armoury was soon complete.

The trader turned to the last horse. It was Nazrah's and like her mistress, a sprightly filly. Tied to her back were ten small wooden containers of honey, still on the comb. This precious commodity had been gathered by Ndorobo hunters and gatherers.

"They are taken to the sacred trees by holy birds of an unknown species. The expert makes a fire beneath these trees," the head of the caravan explained, "and smokes out the bees from deep inside the tree-trunks. The bees fly away, called by Allah, no doubt. Able young men climb up high into the trees, as if pulled up by the holy nectar. The bees are gone, sent away by the celestial smoke. While they are away, the men take the honey from the hive. It is Allah's own sweetness there."

The trader told a tale of magic. One by one, he invited the villagers to sniff the aroma of this delectable delicacy. Hawecha smelled acacia in it and asked shyly how that could be. The caravan leader replied: "The acacia has all the goodness of life in it. The bees know this. And now — because I, Suleiman the trader have brought it to you — you too may know of it!"

The honey disappeared as quickly as everything else had.

Now the horses were loaded with the great rolls of goatskins the villagers had given in barter. Then came many goat-skin bags, all full of sorghum. The last year had yielded a rich harvest and the villagers had put by a goodly store of this staple foodstuff.

Suleiman took a large water-bag from his own horse, drank deeply, signalled to his assistants that business was finished and led his caravan off.

Hawecha watched as they departed in a flurry of dust and importance. They had come to her village, pecked at her people like birds from another land; hurry, hurry, bustle and words. And then ... also like exotic birds ... they had suddenly flown off. Only great piles of horse-dung remained.

# CHAPTER 5

Hawecha grew taller and prettier. She worked hard. The women loved her. But, deep inside her heart, she was not a happy person. Village life kept her busy: milking the cows, looking after goats, or the birth of a young kid. Sunrise and sunset. Day after day. The two other orphans in the settlement were far too young to be her companions. Dawn to dusk, more goats to care for, the birth of a new baby or another cow to milk; would she ever get accustomed to feeling different?

One night, instead of a visitation from Suleh (who came more and more often these days) Hawecha beheld a black horse. It towered over her, filling her field of vision. It took over her whole world.

She remembered the time of the great caravan well, for the tremendous excitement it had brought her. She recalled the odour of horse-dung and the swish-swish of Nazrah's dirty skirts. The horse of her dream was no ordinary beast of burden. It came from beyond this world. On its forehead, there blazed a great light which she immediately recognized as Venus. The horse seemed to speak to her.

"A famine is coming to this part of Liban, a time when there will be nothing to eat. Tell the people, Hawecha. You are the only one who can. Tell them to follow me."

It reared up three times, turned towards the north and galloped away in that direction. It turned its head to make sure she noticed which way it was headed. Then the black horse spoke to her again. "Tell the people to follow." She felt very small as she watched it gallop off.

Hawecha woke from her dream, deeply perplexed. She had learned something of the stars and the lunar calendar which ruled their lives. She had heard of the Women's Star, the War Star and the Elephant Star. She remembered Gababa Halakhe telling her of these. "Had there been a Horse Star?" Hawecha could not remember.

The vision concerned the entire village. Why did the black horse want them all to move? Because of an approaching famine, it had said.

Oromo history was full of stories of great famines, which occurred cyclically over the years. Everybody knew somebody who had lost all their cattle in one, or worse still, a member of the family. Famines were to be dreaded.

Hawecha's heart began to pound.

Where were they supposed to go? North. Her mystical horse had told her so quite clearly. There was no room for error or doubt here. Hawecha knew that Suleh was somehow involved in the creating of this vision. Suleh lived on Venus nowadays ... and had she not seen Venus emblazoned upon the horse's forehead?

The remainder of the night passed with Hawecha trying to grapple with all these troublesome thoughts. They spun round and round in circles. Black horse. Soon. Urgent! Black horse ... famine . . . Suleh. Venus. Famine. FAMINE!

In the morning, she spoke to Galgalu of what she had seen, begging her aunt to listen. Aghast, her aunt related the dream to Jarso. The normally mild-tempered man flew into a great rage. "Your family! What a family you come from! First your mother and now your niece. Who filled her head with such nonsense?" On and on he ranted, until Hawecha felt thoroughly ashamed.

Kneeling down, Galgalu took her by the shoulders, shook her hard, and looked her straight in the eye. "Heavens above, Hawecha, you are far too young to be like Ayo Midadu!" she shouted. "Nor are you another Suleh. Nobody will listen to you! Now, put these dreams away. Go at once and fetch me water!"

Hawecha hung her head. What could she do against the elders? With a heavy heart, she resolved to do as she was told.

# CHAPTER 6

A beautiful, sweet-tempered girl named Salessa was about to get married. Marriage always symbolized new hope for the community, bringing with it the promise of children, laughter and growth. Everyone was greatly excited.

Her parents had chosen a good man for her: strong, and from a family with many cattle. Furthermore, he was good-natured. The marriage boded well. Salessa had six sisters and two brothers. She herself would surely be equally fertile.

Every morning and evening, the old men gathered beneath their Sacred Tree to hold special prayers for the marriage. Once these prayers had been made, the marriage could not be broken.

Then Diima, the bridegroom, came to the village leading the bride price before him: six goats and a white milk cow with beautiful and unusual markings. These he led proudly through the settlement, to his prospective in-laws' home. They were led into the family's livestock enclosure. Everybody came in turn to express their admiration. It was a good bride price: surely, this marriage would be lucky.

Diima returned to his village for the few days he would spend secluded inside his parents' hut. Meanwhile, Salessa too would remain sequestered.

The men met together, discussed and planned for the wedding feast. Each family had to contribute an animal. This goat was chosen to be eaten; this heifer was still too young. "Should I give a goat?" or "Can I be more generous now and give an ox?" These thoughts occupied the men-folk for several days.

Meanwhile, the women were also busy. Each household had to provide a useful gift, such as a ladle or a small wooden cup. Some gave beautiful beads acquired from traders, to enhance Salessa's beauty. One girl, Gatto, was the acknowledged expert in preparing goatskins. She spent four days scraping away at the underside of the skin, to make it soft and supple. This would be her gift to the bride. It would form part of her apparel.

Tumtu, the blacksmith, worked to make the traditional gift from mother to daughter – two twisted iron bracelets which Salessa would wear on her left wrist.

Hawecha watched all these preparations and felt her sorrows melt away. She had had a nightmare, that was all. Only happy days would come upon her village. It was too good a place for any sort of disaster. They formed such a united community.

They needed bright moonlight for the evening festivities. Jarso the Councillor announced that they would wait two days, until the moon was full.

On the day before the wedding, Hawecha re-braided her aunt's hair into the many small plaits that designated a married woman. Her deft fingers flew through the tight black curls as she divided, braided, and divided yet again. Carefully, she wove in the iron ornament that was one of the symbols of marriage. Much pleased with her handiwork, she skipped and twirled about. This was one of her best skills. There were many older women who could not do as well.

The following day, in the late afternoon, everyone gathered in the clearing in the centre of the settlement for the ceremony itself. Poor Hawecha was made to stand at the back of the crowd despite the fact that she was still too short to see much. She caught a glimpse of her uncle's head as he blessed the young couple. She saw the woven grass wreath on Salessa's head. She heard a shout. It seemed the ceremony was over.

Then the cooking began. The smell of roasting goat filled the air. The men-folk huddled inside their huts, being served coffee by their wives or daughters. Every now and then, somebody broke into an ancient song. The stars peeked out from the inky blackness. There was plenty of food.

Tomorrow, Salessa's new family would escort her to her new home in their village to begin her marriage life. This was her last night in her birthplace.

When the eating was done, the women gathered in groups to sing loudly. They had waited all day for this. Their voices rose high and shrill at times. Now and then, a deeper voice held the melody and the high voices provided a chorus. Old verses of goodwill and friendship. Songs of love and joy. Far into the night, the women sang and sang their hearts out.

Hawecha had fetched and carried all day. Her head was weary with 'Do this!' and 'Get that!' Furthermore, her belly was nicely over-filled. At last, she could hold her head up no longer. She found a sandy patch beneath a bush, curled up tight as a kitten and fell exhausted into sleep.

# CHAPTER 7

Alas, the happiness did not last for long! The days grew hotter and hotter. The rains were delayed. Anxiously, the people scanned the skies for the first sign of a rain cloud. White clouds came and went: the leaves on the trees hung listlessly in the stillness. The villagers watched aghast as the grain began to wither on its stalks. The cattle lowed in the middle of the night: "a bad omen," Jarso said.

The river began to shrink. An inch or two and then several feet. Still, the sun grew hotter. Never in living memory had there been such heat! The river was the River of Life, praised in certain prayers. If the river dried up, they would die.

Each morning, Hawecha walked down to the riverbank of her own accord, to check it. Each day, she saw more shrinkage. Clearly, the earth was hurting badly.

The elders gathered the people together to pray for rain, following an ancient custom. The Law demanded two days from them. They prayed to the Water Star, and then they prayed to their ancestors and their five Original Teachers to come and assist them. They watched for omens.

Jarso sensed that one of the men was unclean. Jillo hung his head in shame. He had stolen some food from a neighbour. How he rued his action! Now, he was sent away — never to return to this village. He would henceforth live amongst strangers.

The prayers continued day and night. They took it in turns, so that sore throats could rest. Rest? All throats were parched. The songs became scratchy as voices became hoarse. The two days passed, and still the rain did not come.

Now, seven days of prayer were called for. The people gathered their livestock together, and brought them to the place of prayer. Cattle lowed and stood stoically amongst the crowd. The donkeys swished their tails at the gathering flies and skittered about nervously. The goats were herded together into tight clusters so they could no longer browse. Mothers brought their tiny babies. All the children had to be there. Every single living thing in the entire settlement had to pray for rain. Otherwise, the rain would fail. The rains failed.

A baby cried piteously and died in the midst of a last whimper. Then a young calf succumbed, leaving its mother to bellow in rage. A donkey keeled over and kicked twice in its death-throes.

Jarso remembered that Hawecha had warned him. Why, oh why had he not listened? Now Galgalu comforted him. "She is still young. Who would listen? God chose the wrong messenger. Suleh was wrong too. Nobody listens to an unmarried girl." Still, Jarso wept bitter tears of frustration. Who was he to discredit one whom God had clearly chosen?

The women murmured amongst themselves. "Perhaps she should have told *us*!" Malicha-the-Wise cried. "We are more sensitive than men. Perhaps *we* would have listened!"

Hawecha herself could only sit with a vacant look upon her face as one by one, the people died. The burden was too much for her. Every Oromo girl was brought up to be obedient and subservient to her father's will. Jarso had taken the place of her father. What else could a young girl do? She sat in a small patch of shade, and waited for more suffering.

Twenty seven goats died, bleating feebly in the dust. The men-folk wept. Were the goats not also their children? Given to them by God? They blessed each emaciated corpse. At least there would be a little food for them all.

One day, in the distance, Hawecha saw a small swirl of dust spiral upwards. It spun and spun and as it did so, it grew taller. It grew and grew, until it towered over her head, then it swept through the village, leaving them choking and gasping and coated with dry dust. An evil omen. There was no water to spare for washing it off. Too tired to gather together, they prayed in their huts, each family muttering a few words. All they could do now was to shelter from the blistering heat.

Before dawn, Hawecha walked down to the river for the first time in seven days. She had not dared to look at it. Today, something inside her told her she must. She dragged her feet, afraid of what she would find.

Their great river now lay divided into small puddles. Like her people, she thought. They too lay divided inside their huts, just sitting there like these lifeless puddles. She managed to scoop a little water, muddied by many feet, into the water-pot she had inherited from her mother. She thanked God her mother had not lived to see these terrible times. The people had not listened to her. Too late! Would she always be too late?

As she straightened her back to lift the water-pot onto her head, she heard a by-now familiar voice. Suleh, the one who looked after her: Suleh, the Keeper of Women. "Next time, the people will listen. Next time, you will be old enough." At least Suleh was with her. Suleh who could not die. Suleh had heard her head-talk. Suleh had answered her.

Many people died that year, in this village and in many others. A thousand people, they reckoned, when they counted those who were missing. A terrible loss to the tribe! Only seven families were left now, in this tiny village in the once-great Liban of which Hawecha had been so proud.

Many had moved away to try their luck elsewhere: some had belatedly headed to the north as advised: a few had crossed over to the other side of the river — or over a small hill. Little good it had done them. The famine had fallen upon them all. 'Oh my poor Liban,' Hawecha thought, remembering the teachings of Gababa Halakhe. "What will become of the Oromo people now?"

Hawecha did her own reckoning. Her aunt's best friend, Malicha-the-Wise, had gone. So had her mother's friend Darmi, the Cheerful One. Choleh, her own best friend lived on, but all her youthful joy had gone in nursing her parents. They had not survived. Choleh had aged beyond her years.

Hawecha saw that she had aged too. They said in their oral history that these difficult times were sent to test them-for courage and strength. Those who survived grew quieter and more serious. Perhaps they came closer to God this way? Hawecha had grown quieter, yet she felt no nearer to the Giver of Life. Well, perhaps she was still too young.

A great personal change had fallen upon Hawecha, however. The villagers now recognised her as a Chosen One, one of their ancient lineage. That meant her destiny was not her own to make. She would have to find her own way through the life made for her by the Great Creator. Though still only a girl, they would leave her to find that difficult path.

Now, when she sat quietly, with her head in the stars — or in the clouds — the people treated her with more respect. "Hawecha-the-Dreamer is thinking now. We must leave her to her thinking."

The rains came at the end of the year. The women planted out the few seeds they had managed to husband. Soon small green shoots appeared. The puddles in the river became a small, slow trickle, strung together again at last into something resembling life. The cracks in the shattered earth closed up. The earth began to heal.

People stood outside in the rain, weeping with relief. Their ancestors wept with them from the afterlife world, happy for their children. Once more, a future lay before the Oromo. Many cycles of drought had preceded this one. Each time, the people had survived. With luck, one day they would be great again.

# CHAPTER 8

One day, at the time when the sun beat down directly upon any head that still exposed itself against all known wisdom, a tired donkey ambled into the compound. Upon its back sat a hunched-up personage — fast asleep.

Hawecha had decided to squat beneath a tree and finish her winnowing. Flap, flap! She tossed the grains high into the air and deftly caught them again in her round, flat basket. Swish, swish: she sorted good grain from chaff.

The donkey snuffled at her hair. Hawecha dropped her winnowing basket and gave a shriek of surprise.

"Daughter, take pity on me, a poor and weary traveller."

Awake now, the hunched-up personage had straightened out somewhat, and now addressed Hawecha from atop the donkey. His voice was a mere croak. He pointed to his throat to emphasise his needs. "Milk, daughter .... for pity's sake, a drop of milk!"

Hawecha ran to her aunt's hut and returned with a small calabash. She unstoppered it and poured milk into the flat lid. She saw that the old man — for such it was — could barely hold the cup. In her two hands, she held it gently before him, so he could lower his lips to it.

He sucked greedily and then signalled for more. Hawecha filled the cup again. The stranger wiped his mouth with the back of his hand and thanked Hawecha for her kindness.

"I have come from far, my daughter. I seek a place to live in. Do you think this village would be good for me? I am old and quite worn out. I need a good, quiet home now."

Hawecha studied him intently. His hump had been partly a physical deformity. Even now, having recovered his strength to some extent, he could not sit straight upon his donkey. The folds of skin lay deep around his neck. His shoulder-blades stuck out and his arms were scrawny.

Gazing into his eyes, deep-set beneath furrows and creases, Hawecha saw that they twinkled. A kindly man, indeed.

"I am sure you are most welcome, venerated sir. Our village grew small in the famine. Every human being is needed."

The old man's shoulders shook with amusement. "I cannot add to the grandeur of this homestead. I am too old to give you children." Hawecha understood that this was so.

"No harm, sir. No harm at all. We need a few wise heads here also. Many of our dear ones have gone."

She helped him down from his donkey.

"I will take you to the home of our ritual leader. He will look after you."

It transpired that Dabassah was a herbalist of great repute and also a thrower-of-sandals. After a night of rest with the head family, he asked to be taken to the holy tree.

"We will revive it." he announced. "Notify the villagers and I will tell them who I am."

One by one, they gathered. Dabassah introduced himself but because he was so old, he could not stand for long and address them. A small wooden stool was brought for him to sit upon. He laid down his staff upon the ground, near to hand, in case he decided to use it.

"I come from a long line of herbalists," he began. "My father was one and so was his father before him. Since time began, my family has always produced one great herbalist from amongst their many sons."

The villagers nodded in agreement. Stories of ancient lineages were well known to them. Duties and skills were often of a hereditary nature. They waited for him to continue.

"Alas, I am the very last of this great line. I have no children to follow me. I am what you see before you. Nobody stands behind me."

What an unusual situation. How terrible to have no children. The women moaned and sighed for him: the men-folk rocked backwards and forwards on their haunches, as if they too could feel the lack, the loss and the pain of it.

"I began my life in the shade of Mount Abuna. I am sure you all know it. It is our holiest place. Some call it the Holy of Holies."

Everybody nodded.

"I have healed the sick for many years. Many upon many have been healed by me. When my father died, I moved south to Tuqqa. There, I lived for many years, healing many, many more."

In view of his very great age, nobody could doubt this.

"Later on, I felt pulled by Venus to move to another place. I took up my belongings and rode my donkey all the way from Tuqqa to the north again. I ended up in Arero."

It was not the custom to interrupt an elder once he had started speaking. Although all were more interested in the matter of his fortune-telling and his sandals, they waited patiently for him to arrive at this point in his story.

"I know all the herbs from the low hills of our land and I also know many that grow higher up on mountain slopes. I am familiar with the plants that grow along our rivers. I have collected herbs near the River Ganale and I have also studied those that grow along the banks of your own river, the River Dawa . . . but further to the east than where we sit now. I have studied many kinds of medicines — from trees, shrubs and small plants. My father taught me very well indeed."

A child yawned. Another simply nodded off.

"One day, a diviner came to Tuqqa."

Here at last was the promised joy. Everyone perked up.

"A venerable sage, who knew much. God had favoured him. He knew about numbers and about stars. But what he was best known for was his skill with the throwing of sandals.

"From this great man, I learned a noble art. He told me I excelled. Nevertheless, it took me seven years to learn all that pertains to this form of divination."

Imagine, seven years of learning. And just for throwing two sandals upon the ground! Who would have the patience?

Hawecha smiled broadly. Since Gababa Halakhe had left them all, she had been bereft of spiritual wisdom. Here before her at last, stood another wondrous spirit full of the knowledge of the ages.

The old man continued his dissertation.

"I am vastly skilled in divination and I know much about the plants. What I do not know is which medicines I can provide for you. If you allow me to remain here."

There was nobody present who did not want this noble addition to their village. Indeed, he would bring much honour upon them. They all made haste to assure him that he was most welcome.

"I have not many years left, you know," he reminded them. "I wish to spend them in a good and quiet place, far removed from worldly matters. I thank you for letting me stay."

The elders reiterated their welcome. A hut would be built for him in due course. Meanwhile, he would be the guest of the ritual leader. All was well. It had already been agreed upon.

"In the matter of the medicines," old Dabassah resumed, "I shall ask the youngsters to take me for a walk around this place, once I have had my rest. I need to see what grows here, you know. This is a new place for me."

He turned sideways so that all could see his profile. "You see my hump, children?" some nodded, whilst others closed their eyes in embarrassment. "This is a sign of age. I have learned to live with it. You see, looking for herbal remedies can be quite hard work. It is no good looking for them up in the air." He gesticulated in that direction. "I carry my hump with me every day. It came to me late in life and I at last see the wisdom of it. It keeps my nose closer to the ground."

What a saintly character. And one who could laugh at himself. The villagers decided he was a gift from heaven. They fell in love with him at once.

# CHAPTER 9

Hawecha, Choleh and a strong lad called Boru-The-Big-One, all volunteered to 'show the Old One around'.

"I rise early, just like the birds," Dabassah announced. "The plants must be fresh when we find them, not covered with dust, or bowed down with heat."

Shortly after dawn, they stood outside the ritual leader's hut. Dabassah appeared, staff in hand, looking fresher and slightly younger than he had the day before. They set off with him in the lead and the three children marched joyously behind him. He had a way with young ones, it was clear. The parents watched them set off on their quest. The villagers were like a family. It was good to have a new member come amongst them.

Dabassah pointed to various items of interest as they trailed along the well known paths. "See, here a snail has gone for a walk." He showed them. "Those two beautiful birds with purple breasts and greenish feathers upon their backs have come to bring good news." The children marvelled at the Lilac-Breasted Rollers that had settled atop a thornbush. He cocked his head to listen. "They say we will find things." Hunch backed he might be, but there was nothing wrong with his eyes or his hidden senses.

Shortly afterwards, he stopped beside a small shrub. "I know this one," he announced triumphantly. "The roots are for healing warts. Perhaps it is not the most useful of all the plants that grow in our world but, nevertheless, it will do."

A little later on, he brought them up abruptly in front of a low and leafy bush. "Aha! Now I am truly pleased." It transpired that this was one of the best medicinal plants in the whole wide world. It was to help women through their periods, when so many of them suffered from cramps. Hawecha did, though not badly. So did Choleh — only more so. The girls looked at each other and smiled. At last, they would find relief. Poor Boru knew little of menstrual problems, this being a subject forbidden to boys. Nevertheless, he had some faint inklings of what women went through. He turned away and scuffed at the dirt, making himself appear terribly, terribly busy.

By that time, Dabassah was visibly tired. "We will continue another day. Meanwhile, you have all seen what I want. When the time comes, you will collect them for me, won't you?"

How could they refuse?

Over the subsequent week or so, they made several forays in different directions. A walk along the river banks revealed nothing that was useful. A long, slow amble through the nearby savannah was equally unrewarding.

Just as the children were giving up hope of building up a good and reliable stock of remedies, Dabassah paused dramatically, with one foot in the air and pounced upon a low, lowly plant that seemed to cower beneath a higher one.

"Aha!" The children loved his exuberance and looked forward enormously to his "Aha!"

"We have found a treasure here. Look thou well upon it!" They had noticed that every now and then his speech became a little archaic. He used words they did not know — or more words than were needed. Obediently, they crouched down to admire what his stick was pointing at. To their eyes it was quite unremarkable. It had no bright flowers, no bees to buzz around it. It was, quite simply, a plant. Hawecha screwed up her eyes in disappointment.

"Here before you is a great gift. It reaches far into your belly and sucks out all the pain there. When you have eaten too much, or have swallowed something not good for you, this .... this! .... will simply pull it out!" They were carried away by his enthusiasm.

Dabassah decided to retrace their steps carefully but this time searching upwards. He told the children to look above his shoulders whenever they passed beneath a tree. He himself could not raise his head so high. They were to describe to him what they saw there. A Raven, a Yellow-Billed Shrike, what did he mean, then?

It was Choleh who found it: a clump of growth on a low branch, a parasitic plant that had attached itself to a parent. Another "Aha!" came from Dabassah.

"We are doing well, my friends, very well indeed." He smiled a smile of the deepest satisfaction. "This will heal liver ailments if I use it carefully. And I am always, always, careful."

Boru was appointed to climb up the tree one day, armed with a very sharp knife, to cut out the 'whole caboodle' and bring it home to be cooked. "It must be boiled and boiled, you see," Dabassah informed the novices. "It tastes quite bad, but it is quickly swallowed. And then comes the magic of the cure."

On their last field trip, down to the water and back again, Dabassah shook his head disconsolately. "Alas that you have such small hills here. A large hill is the mother of many medicines." He tut-tutted in disapproval. "I will of course make use of whatever I can find for you all, but it is little, oh so very little." He stopped in his tracks, shrugged his shoulders and resumed his forward march (a majestic and slow-paced one, of course, commensurate with age and wisdom).

"Perhaps I will have better luck with the sandals after all," he announced quite suddenly, stopping dead in his tracks yet again. The children all bumped into each other and into him. They resumed their walk with as much dignity as they could muster.

A clump of bushes stood not far off, all higgledy-piggledy a-jumble. Dabassah made straight for it and proceeded to poke about with his stick, separating this one from that one. Hidden deep inside, he revealed a small shrub with dark green, shiny leaves. "Pneumonia!" he pronounced delightedly. "And indeed all chest complaints. The birds were right. My troubles are over now!"

It seemed that they were, for shortly thereafter, his attention was caught by a few seed-pods that hung in the air at breast level — hence easily found.

"Oh my goodness, the greatest treasure of them all!"

He plucked a few and stuffed them into a small leather pouch at his waist. "Too good to be true." He set off mumbling happily to himself, chortling and chuckling.

Hawecha ran up beside him and took him by the elbow. "What is it, grandfather? You haven't explained it to us. Do tell!"

*"Horsissa!"*

"What does it do?"

Instead of answering, Dabassah burst into loud barks of laughter, which shook his thin body from top to toe. He rocked on his heels, trying to keep his balance. Only his stout staff saved him from total collapse.

He set off towards the village, still shaking and quaking in his mirth. "You'd better ask your uncle." Once more, loud cackles prevented further conversation. Hawecha shrugged her shoulders, in fond imitation of the sage, and turned to her friend Choleh.

"We'll both ask him together."

The girls trotted off after the old man. When they neared the village gate, Dabassah drew Hawecha aside. He sat down on a stool in the sunshine and gently pulled her to him.

"Don't be afraid of me, Hawecha. I only want to see what I see in you." She calmly returned his gaze.

Saying nothing, he shooed her off. Then he arose and went inside the hut to discuss the matter with Buleh — The-Ritual-Leader. Buleh was a kindly man, but — as has been said — in his dotage and a bit confused in his thinking.

"She is a thinker, our Hawecha," old Dabassah began. "You and I are very old indeed now. Our turn will soon come to leave this world. We must begin to focus on the other one."

"What? What! Oh, yes .... What?" was all that Buleh could deliver by way of expected response.

Dabassah decided he should talk to Jarso, a much younger and fitter man. And her guardian, to boot. Grumbling a bit at the ache in his bones, he went through all the complex manoeuvres necessary to the removal of his body from one place to another, adjusted his staff, and set out for Jarso's hut.

"She is a thinker," he began again and repeated his thoughts on the after world. "Those of us who see what others cannot see have a great responsibility. We have to choose those best suited to follow in our learned footsteps. We have to create the next generation of sages."

Jarso was much impressed by the fact that Dabassah trusted him with such a weighty matter. He drew himself up, to appear taller and wiser, and nodded his agreement.

"I cannot see everything, you understand." Jarso nodded again. "All I see is that she has a gift. It lies there in her eyes. She has that far-away look that all seers have." Dabassah shuffled his feet about in the dirt and ahemmed three times.

"Pride! That is what we must watch out for. If we tell her this now, she will be lost to posterity. She must remain simple and pure for as long as is possible."

Jarso saw the wisdom in this and again nodded in support.

"She foresaw the coming of the famine. That is an excellent sign. She told you what she saw; that is a better one, for it shows her desire to obey you. My counsel is that you bide your time. Let her grow up in the normal way. One day, she will awaken to her powers. Meanwhile, we must work to keep her practical and normal."

Jarso had expected nothing less from his adopted daughter. He hoped she would look after him in his old age, or take care of Galgalu when he had gone. He quailed at the very idea of another seer in the family. For his part, he would quash her very spirit if he had to.

Dabassah was shrewd and wise in the ways of men. "She is already spoken of as a soothsayer. You cannot stem the flow of the river once the flood has commenced." They agreed to watch her carefully, and await further developments.

That evening, Hawecha and Choleh sidled into the hut and stood there hand in hand before Jarso. It was Hawecha who finally plucked up sufficient courage to ask him what *horsissa* was. "He told us to ask you, uncle. Truly, he did."

Jarso could not reply. He was caught between a great explosion of laughter and a desire to maintain the demeanour appropriate to a councillor. In the end, he waved both arms about in a most undignified manner and advised them to ask Galgalu. She too was overcome with mirth.

What could the mysterious seed-pods possibly contain? Would nobody enlighten them? One by one, the two girls posed the question before several of the younger men and several of the older women. "But he told us to," drew no response, other than hee-haws, snickers and nudgings. At last, Choleh suggested they ask Jillo the midwife. "We've tried almost everyone else!"

Jillo laughed outrageously, just as everyone else had. In the end, she wheezed and gasped and made a tremendous pronouncement. "*Horsissa* is all about having babies. It is something a man must have in order to become a father. It's not a physical thing, you understand. I'm sure you've both seen plenty of that."

Both girls had of course. With cows and bulls about and she-goats and he-goats, the facts of life were fairly obvious.

"This is a hidden power. Some men have it and some, alas, do not. Those that do not, could put me out of business. Who would pay me goats for all my work, if it were not for male virility?" The girls thought they understood a little bit more now.

"One day, you will learn more about it. Until then, don't tell anyone I told you. The men would kill me if they knew!" Hawecha and Choleh — despite their curiosity — vowed eternal silence.

As for Boru, it seemed he had acquired some insights from another source. Whenever he bumped into the two girls he would hang his head and mutter something about having been sent on an urgent errand.

That day became a part of local history. It was not remembered as 'The Day of the Sixth Herb,' nor as 'The Day of the Talk between Jarso and Dabassah'. Yet, it was talked about for many, many moons.

Whenever it was mentioned, somebody burst out laughing. They gave it the most appropriate name they could think of. They called it 'The Day of the Great Laugh'.

# CHAPTER 10

It took four years for the settlement to recover fully from the famine. Once more, marriages could be arranged. New babies were born. Young kids bleated again in the homesteads, or nuzzled their mothers for milk. The milk came in plentiful supply. The new babies grew fat.

Hawecha was now sixteen. Tall, lithe and very beautiful. She held herself erect. If she was a Chosen One, she would stand tall even if the path through life was hard. She understood that life moved in great cycles, of plenty and then of nothing. It seemed that was the way to grow in spirit.

There was physical development as well. The men-folk had their age-set system to help them move from child to boy, to warrior, protector and then to elder. Perhaps a leader.

She saw that for women the way was different; through marriage and motherhood, yes, but also through quietness, guidance and observation. There were a few great women in their history. Each had found her strength and wisdom: midwives, healers, story-tellers. She wondered what her own role would be.

Meanwhile, there were endless chores to keep her busy. Pounding grain, collecting firewood, holding babies, helping others, fetching and carrying. Life was a day-to-day chore, from dawn to dusk and often well beyond that. There was little time for thinking. Jarso kept his promise to Dabassah to make her work hard and often harder than anyone else did.

Her friend Choleh was betrothed to a quiet young man called Harero. She was shy about it, but it was clearly a case of love. She had presented her case to her parents and there had been no opposition. Everyone admired Harero. He was intelligent, well-intentioned and always sought to make himself useful. After the respective fathers had discussed the bride price, once more, a wedding took place, auguring well for the future of the tribe.

Shortly afterwards it was the turn of Zugura, an outspoken girl, who had always known what she wanted. Hers was an arranged marriage, and the choice had been made by her father. The bridegroom came from a pious family. It was hoped that Zugura would put some 'sparkle' into him and make him a little more down to earth. Meanwhile, he would soften her personality somewhat and make her more friendly and easy to get along with.

One by one, all the girls of marriageable age were embarking on their lives as wives and mothers. People began to look at Hawecha. When would she get married?

This was a problem that had long troubled Jarso. As both her uncle and a councillor, his responsibility was to make a good choice for her. She came from an old and respected family on her mother's side and an even older one on her father's. She was obedient, skilled in women's work and beautiful. Yet it was not easy to marry her off. She was too quiet, shy and introspective. She was Hawecha-the-Dreamer. She did not know how to flirt, or twirl seductively in front of a man. She laughed seldom — although her smile was charming and filled her face with light. But who could see her smile, when she held her head down and smiled at the ground in front of a man? She had become attached to old Dabassah and when time permitted, followed him about the village plying him with questions.

It transpired that he knew little about the stars and not much about the Oromo calendar. As long as she confined her questions to medicinal plants, he was pleased to pay her attention. More often than not, however, he was inclined to tell her not to bother him. He too was keeping his side of the bargain with Jarso.

As for the councillor, he was much given to sighing repeatedly. The matter of Hawecha's marriage troubled him greatly. She was not an easy thing for a young and virile man to live with. And so, Jarso pondered and plotted, reaching nowhere.

Choleh produced a laughing daughter, whom they called Diramu because she was born at dawn. Hawecha was thrilled to see her friend so happy and adored the chubby, chortling child.

"What about you, Hawecha?" Choleh teased. "When will you have a baby?"

Hawecha confided that she hoped to marry one day, but didn't know who would want her. Suleh had not married. Perhaps — sadly — marriage was not for her either. Choleh grew angry and said she was wrong. Suleh was the only unmarried woman in their history. One day, Hawecha would surely marry.

Another Somali caravan came their way, their horses laden with glass beads and trinkets, salt and iron. One young man wanted to stay. He was tired of endless roaming. He had been a trader simply because his father had been one, yet he had no natural aptitude for it. It seemed he had long yearned to become a pastoralist. His parents had died and he was old enough to make his own decisions.

Mehmet had fallen in love with Taditi at first sight. He asked old Buleh-The-Ritual-Leader for permission to remain and learn their ways. His manner was humble. Buleh, who was not too senile when it came to a matter of marriage and progeny, decided if Taditi were willing and if her parents approved, he himself would have no objections.

The matter of religion was quickly disposed of. Memetti, as he was called by the Oromo, announced that he much preferred the ways of the Oromo God, finding this Father to be a much kinder one. He also felt the Oromo were more innocent, more gentle and closer to a truly religious life than his own people were.

He married Taditi. In time, a lusty boy was born; new blood for the community. Surely he would be the proud ancestor of many lusty boys.

Galgalu sat in silent calculation. Hawecha had been born after the birth of twins in the village, but before the greatest harvest they all remembered. She decided that Hawecha was eighteen — a shocking age to remain without a husband. She goaded Jarso into taking urgent action.

Jarso saw that he would have to make a decision. Any decision. The Law required every woman to be married and he had to uphold the Law. Hawecha, for all her peculiarities, was undoubtedly a woman. He saddled his horse, took his 'stick of authority', and rode off 'in all directions,' announcing that he would only return once his choice was made.

Hawecha watched as he headed towards the west, wondering what he would find there.

# CHAPTER 11

Three weeks later, Jarso returned, with many tales of the relatives he had visited and the stories he had heard. The news from far north was interesting. Ras Yemariam Bariyaw had rebelled against the Emperor Ioas. The Oromo were a law unto themselves, confining their territory to Liban. Yet whatever happened to their neighbours would eventually have an influence upon their lives. It was good to keep in touch.

Rapidly, a crowd gathered around him. On and on he spoke exaggerating every detail, of course. Six thousand horses belonging to Ras Sihul Mikael had been mustered to help quell the rebellion. "More likely six hundred," Hawecha thought as she bristled angrily in the shadows. Had he entirely forgotten his true purpose in the journey? Never mind the news. What about his duty to her?

The price of grain was thus and so ... No, he had been unable to find beads for the women. As each question was asked, he answered at great (and unnecessary) length. This had been the most interesting of his more recent journeys. He wished to boast and make the most of it.

At last, the crowd fell back, called one by one to their duties. Jarso unsaddled his horse, went into the hut and threw himself down upon his bed of goatskins. "Water, Galgalu. Bring me a great quaff of water, for I have built up a very great thirst." Galgalu grimaced. She took a wooden cup and filled it from the giraffe-neck water container which stood near the doorway.

Jarso quaffed and slurped and quaffed some more: then demanded a second filling. Galgalu could contain herself no longer. "And Hawecha, who stands here beside me? Have you nothing to tell us for her? Truly, you try a woman's patience."

Her husband was filled with remorse. To bring news of far away war was part of his duty but finding a husband for his wife's niece was equally his duty. "Forgive me, both of you. I have been too much the councillor."

Much mollified, Galgalu and Hawecha sat down upon their wooden stools prepared to listen.

Jarso explained that in the course of his travels he had met three likely candidates. He had pressed suit on her behalf and all three sets of parents were interested. Then, he had gone off quietly by himself for a day — tearing himself away from coffee, friends and rest, he pointed out — in order to think the matter through. One young man was handsome and well-thought-of, another one was very pious, but ugly to look upon and the third was from a wealthy family, blessed with many cows and goats: the son of a lucky trader.

"In the end, I chose the rich man's son," he announced. "If Hawecha is to be a Dreamer, then at least let her husband give her some material comfort."

Galgalu was overjoyed, and ran out to tell the other women. Jarso placed his hand on Hawecha's shoulder, as she bent to refill his cup. "Blessings be upon you. I am much relieved."

The news spread swiftly. "Hawecha is to be married!"

Choleh came, with a small gift of salt. "It is all I have at the moment." One by one, the young girls and the young married women came to congratulate her. This was Hawecha's day! Never had she felt so beloved, so queenly. She smiled into people's eyes for the first time. All could see her pride. At last, she too would be married.

Juldess arrived two days later and the whole village turned out to greet him. Oh, he was a handsome lad. Look, how tall and well-built! His horse was a good one. His manners were ingratiating. Furthermore, he radiated confidence. They all felt Hawecha had done well for herself. The men told Jarso he was a wise one.

Only Galgalu noticed how he looked at Jillo, how he smiled at Qooyeh and how he flirted openly with the seductive daughter of Boro. She kept her misgivings to herself, however. "It will pass," she thought. "He knows he is good-looking and he is still so young. Once they are married, all will go well." She quieted her beating heart. As for Hawecha, she was completely overwhelmed. She at once fell utterly in love.

Juldess had been told much about her. How dutiful she was and how beautiful, which interested him more. "She will make you proud." Jarso had said. "One day, she will be a leader." Now she stood before him, head downcast, a bit too modest for his liking. Slim, yes, with neat little feet. But so shy. He wondered what she would be like 'under the goatskins' as they said. "Not much," he thought to himself. Yet his father had warned him that he had to marry this one. He had flirted with too many.

Events moved on apace. The elders prayed to bless the union. Juldess brought the bride price: three horses and seven cows. Now Jarso was a wealthy man. He puffed himself up with pride.

The days of seclusion came. On the morning of the wedding day, Juldess came to visit Galgalu, who took the place of Hawecha's mother on this occasion. As custom dictated, Galgalu milked a cow and proceeded to make the ceremonial coffee in the special coffee bowl. Several men, including Juldess and his father, Harkalo, came into the hut to join them in the prayers and the drinking.

Juldess' mother had not come for the wedding. She had trodden on a thorn and her foot was infected. Hawecha was nervous of meeting her later on. She kept her head down as she passed the cup from one to another, to hide her anxiety. As she passed the cup to Juldess, he thought sadly of the end of freedom.

The villagers, on the other hand, were overjoyed to have yet another reason to celebrate. The population had grown enormously. They now numbered more than sixty and there were many new huts alongside the original sixteen of Hawecha's childhood. But there was always room for more.

Hawecha's thoughts were all upon her marriage night. She was terribly worried. Her aunt had long ago explained the facts of life to her. She had often seen male genitals peeking out through goatskins. Surely, all would go well for her? "It might hurt a little the first time," her aunt had said. Hawecha wondered how much was 'a little'. Whereas her uncle always exaggerated, Galgalu underplayed events and was more philosophical. It would probably hurt more than just 'a little'.

The women dressed her in three new goatskins: soft, pliant and seductive. They placed the woven grass wreath upon her head. Galgalu put two iron bracelets on her left wrist. Hawecha' s thoughts flew back to all the weddings she had witnessed. Her friends all looked pleased with life. Marriage was deemed to be a blessing. Juldess looked guilty, but few noticed.

As usual, the singing went on well into the night. This time, Hawecha stayed up to listen. It was the last night she would spend in her homestead. She wanted to live every moment.

In the morning, the goodbyes were brief. It was harvest time and everyone was busy. Harkalo came up to her, astride a black and powerful horse. "Bought from the Portuguese," it was said.

Everyone knew that, over a period of many, many years, three great religions had been introduced to the northern part of Ethiopia. These were Judaism, Islam and Christianity.

The Muslims under a great warlord dubbed Gragn (meaning left-handed) had swept across the Christianised territories over two hundred years earlier, in the 1540s. Eventually, the Christian Emperor, Gelawdewos, had sent emissaries to the King of Portugal, requesting assistance. Gragn was defeated in a great battle but was able to obtain armed help from the Turks. A decisive battle between Christian and Muslim forces had taken place in 1543: Gragn was defeated and the Christian Emperor once more resumed power.

After fifteen years of bloodshed, the country was badly weakened. The Oromo had taken this opportunity to expand their own pastureland enormously, moving to both the south and west.

Hawecha had heard of the Portuguese, those long-ago visitors to the north, who were all Christians. She had been told by her mother that their skins were sickly in colour, rather like milk that had curdled and gone sour. They wore strange leather sandals upon their feet, which encased their legs up to their knees. These strange objects were identified as 'boots'. Legends described them as being extraordinarily hirsute, with body hair all over.

By far the strangest fact about them was the fact that, in small pouches tied to their waists, they kept something metallic that jingled loudly. This was known as 'money' and was divided up into something called 'coins'. To the Oromo — who had no need of money, using their livestock to barter for whatever they needed — this 'money' seemed a most peculiar invention.

The Portuguese had introduced a new breed of horse, which had been interbred with the smaller local breed. The thoroughbred lines still told, however. They were evident in the black horse upon which Hawecha's father-in-law now sat. It snorted as she eyed it warily. Juldess' own mount reared up and pawed at the air.

They had brought a small brown mare for Hawecha to ride on, skittish and not overly friendly. Hawecha was a little afraid of horses, preferring lowly donkeys instead. Those patient beasts of burden had long ago won her heart. Horses were noble, undoubtedly ... but, oh, they scared her!

There was a pause whilst she tied on her few bundles. In one goatskin, she had wrapped the wooden ceremonial coffee bowl her mother had left to her; of all a woman's possessions, this bowl was considered the most important. In another she had placed her small wooden bowls, ladles and cups. Next came a bundle of thongs, some wide leather straps and her sandals, which she hated to wear, much preferring the feel of good earth beneath her feet.

Another bundle contained her mother's ceremonial ornaments: the back apron fringed with small gourd-tops, that clacked together with every movement and the special wrist-ornament, also hung with the clacking gourd-tops.

In a pouch around her waist she had put her mother's iron shoulder-ornament worn only by wives of Elders who had reached the tenth age-set. It was a large round boss, with a raised phallic symbol at its centre. Around this were three concentric circles of pierced holes. A criss-cross design was etched around the edge.

Hawecha's mother had inherited it from her mother, but of course had never worn it; her husband having died too young. For many generations it had been handed down from mother to daughter at the mother's death. Hawecha prayed that one day she would wear it. In any case, she would pass the precious shoulder-ornament on to someone else. She liked the idea of continuity.

As she packed her belongings, Hawecha wondered what other novelties all the northern invaders had brought to her people, apart from new religions. Living as far south as they did, only a few innovations came to their attention. Yet, these few could destroy Oromo culture if allowed to do so. Money? Boots? Large horses? What next? These thoughts made Hawecha sad.

The mare tossed its head, and turned around to nip her. Hawecha persevered, praying to Suleh to help her. All the bundles were tied on now. There was no excuse to delay. She hugged Choleh who had insisted on seeing her off. "It's only a short walk away," Choleh grinned. "I will see you often."

"Three miles," Hawecha thought. "Not so short a walk on a hot day. And too far for some."

She mounted the mare and signalled that she was ready. Trying to maintain her dignity and the demeanour of a properly married woman, she trotted off behind her new husband and her in-law.

# CHAPTER 12

The ride was long and wearisome. The three miles to her new home seemed endless: perhaps because she was afraid to get there. Harkalo spoke not at all, simply assuming she would keep up with him. She did — just — slipping from left to right in her 'saddle', a folded goatskin tied on firmly with ropes made from tough fibres. The 'stirrups' (made of ropes) were too long for her. Her feet dangled down loosely to either side. No wonder she could not keep straight. Juldess rode ahead, ignoring her completely.

Over the flat plains they travelled, as the sun rose higher and higher. Far to the left lay large fields of sorghum, promising a good harvest this year. In the distance to the right, she could see a few flat-topped thorn trees. Between the path and the trees, the ground was grassy but stony. The mare stumbled once or twice. Hawecha righted herself, hitched her goatskin skirt a little higher, and decided to while away the time in thinking of other matters.

She fingered the small flat leather pouch around her neck, her talisman for good luck. A friend of her aunt's had made it specially for her. Inside were all sorts of 'medicines': crushed seeds, a small dried berry, a bit of dirt from the floor of the hut, a minute scrap of goatskin, a shred of bark and spit. Of all these, she suspected the spit was the most powerful protection. After all, Godanna was a powerful woman!

Her thoughts turned to the five High Priests who governed the spiritual welfare of the people. Did they too wear amulets and if so what was contained in them? She allowed her mind to explore other spiritual questions.

Old Gababa Halakhe had told the children that the Five First Teachers had come from the stars: three from the Pleiades. He had known of one that had come from Venus and one that swore he had been born on Sirius. "That was the time when men wore wings!" Her old teacher had said. Had she come from a star? It was said that if you had, you would certainly know it. She loved the stars so much and felt such a kinship with them. She closed her eyes briefly and asked the stars to speak to her. One star. If she had come from one of those bright twinkles, now was the time to find out.

"I am Sirius, the brightest star of all stars." She heard a male voice inside her head. "This is where you were born, Hawecha. But long, long ago. You went to earth to see what it was like. One day, you will tell your star-companions all about it."

Hawecha smiled. Of course her home had been on Sirius. She always found herself searching for it in the night skies and grew melancholy in the months when it was not visible overhead. "It is visiting the Dogon people in Mali at those times," old Halakhe had explained.

Once upon a time, it seemed, the Dogon and the Oromo had been one and the same people. Something — she forgot what — had happened to divide the tribe. It was after Egypt. Half the people had decided to migrate southwards, whilst the other half had headed towards the west. "They have the same stars as we do: the stars still link us together."

Ahead of her now, she saw a large cluster of huts, protected by the usual thornbush enclosure. Her new home. She was going to face so very many strangers. Harkalo dismounted and helped her down. Not so dour as he seemed, then. Hawecha smiled timidly and thanked him.

Small children came running out of the gateway to greet her, jumping up and down in their excitement. A sweet girl of six or seven, wearing nothing but a carnelian bead on a thong around her neck, broke into a song, of welcome, her thin high treble piercing the hot air just like ... like ... like a star piercing the darkness of night,' Hawecha thought. She hugged the child, delighted to have at once made such a friend.

Juldess's mother — a tall and graceful woman called Guyatu-Mother-Of-One beckoned from inside the gateway, greeted Hawecha pleasantly and hobbled back to her hut, inviting Hawecha inside to rest. The round hut was much larger than Jarso's had been. But then, she had married the son of a wealthy man. Hawecha looked about her.

On the rear wall hung three long narrow leather panels, all decorated with white cowrie shells. These symbolized the home and fertility.

Hawecha' s mother had been too poor to afford cowries, which came to them via traders from distant lands. These were the finest leather panels Hawecha had seen. She walked close to inspect the handiwork. The stitches were incredibly neat and orderly, marching in straight lines along the back of the panels, holding each cowrie in place. The design itself was unusual: a clan marking? Or perhaps one special to this family?

Guyatu smiled. "They were made by my mother's hands," she explained, delighted to see her daughter-in-law take such an interest.

Hawecha sat down on a low stool and arched her back, grown a little cramped from jogging up and down on the skittish mare. Guyatu lit the fire and made coffee for them both, in a private welcoming ceremony. She needed help in the house and saw from Hawecha's neat appearance that the help would be forthcoming. She noticed the long, slim fingers and the deftness with which Hawecha took the wooden cup.

So, she was a Dreamer. Was she destined perhaps for greatness? Well, marriage would settle her down and give her the proper background. They would bask in her success, perhaps? Guyatu nodded her head as her inner conversation continued. Yes, this marriage would work. Juldess was the very treasure of her heart. How could the marriage not be a good one?

Hawecha's eyes roamed about the hut, admiring the utensils carefully propped against the walls. There were several small round woven mats made from wild grasses and from leaves. These were useful as trays for serving food to strangers. There were two winnowing baskets nearby, three covered wooden pots and a large pot with no lid; a beautiful large clay water-jug, and a very small one. Nearby lay the essential coffee-bowl. On a small shelf of branches sat three narrow-necked calabashes, with simple decorative patterns burned into them with a hot iron rod.

In another area, she noticed two iron digging sticks and a large iron scythe. The blade was visibly sharp; it glinted as a shaft of sunlight penetrated the loosely woven walls of the hut.

Overhead hung the large rounded milk container used only in ceremonies. Next to it hung a pair of cleverly made scales: two small leather bags hung at either end of a short length of wood. Ah yes, the sign of a trader.

In a corner, next to the sleeping area, was a small open bower, put together from small stripped branches, arched and lashed together. Inside this, the women burned incense, used before all ceremonies as a purification.

All was exceptionally orderly. Hawecha rejoiced. Her mother-in-law was like herself then: there was nothing to fear here. She longed to set up her own home and arrange the few belongings that had come to her from her mother. Her wedding gifts had been loaded onto Harkalo's great horse. How exciting! She wondered where her new home was to be.

They had built a new hut for the married couple, on the edge of the settlement, far from the central ritual hut — the House of Ceremonies. Hawecha was glad. She wished to remain quietly on the periphery until she had settled in. When the babies came, perhaps she and Juldess would be allocated a more central position. She blushed at the thought of babies.

At last, she had unwrapped her treasures and put them exactly where she wanted them. She sat down beside the hearth stones Guyatu had provided and imagined all the many meals she would prepare there. She looked fondly at the heavy grinding stone which had been her mother's and which Harkalo had carried for her on his horse. Yes, there would be tons of sorghum ground upon it.

A head peeked round the doorway: the little girl with the carnelian talisman. "My name is Darmi," the girl announced with not a trace of shyness. "May I sweep the house for you?" Hawecha gave her one of her rare and beautiful smiles which turned her eyes into pools of starbright. "My sweetheart, the house is all in order today. Perhaps tomorrow you may help me." The little girl twirled about and trotted off. Hawecha thought of the other Darmi, her mother's closest friend, also bright and cheerful and endlessly in awe of the magic that was life.

Dusk came upon her and with it came her husband Juldess. He flashed her a smile of great confidence, grabbed her hard and kissed her. She felt at once how he wanted her. This was her marriage night. Despite the 'just a little pain' her aunt had warned of, Hawecha was determined to try to please him. She responded by slackening her tense muscles. Again he kissed her ardently. Was she not to prepare a meal for him? Or roast coffee beans for a ceremonial drink? Not even a cup of water?

It seemed not. He steered her towards the bed of branches, upon which she had neatly laid the goatskins. Grinning wildly, he thrust her back upon the bed and hungrily tore apart her shoulder-wrap, exposing her neat young-woman breasts. He suckled them one by one. Hawecha was not sure that she enjoyed this. Was a man not to be a man then? Why did he behave like a new baby? Then, as her nipples hardened she understood the why of it.

As he ripped off his own goatskin wrap, Hawecha realised the sun was setting. Her mind was now bound to Juldess. Her heart and soul were his. The sun had set upon a young girl. Tomorrow, it would rise upon a woman.

# CHAPTER 13

Hawecha stirred. Her first morning beside her husband. She sighed and rolled over. Oh, how she ached! Three times, Juldess had taken her in the night and each time it had hurt more than 'just a little'. She wondered if she would ever walk again. Were all young men so lusty?

A cock crew vociferously, with all its male pride and vigour. She opened her eyes. The space beside her was empty. She sat bolt upright in shock. How dared he leave her alone right now? And without his morning meal? Was she not to perform her duties as a housewife? She herself was starving. Grouchily, she rose from the low bed, stretched, yawned and looked about her. Her new home. Not much of a home, without a husband in it.

Hawecha performed her ablutions, revolted at the dried blood upon her thighs. The truth of the marriage night was far worse than any stories. She was thankful for the full water-pot her mother-in-law had thoughtfully provided. At least she could avoid having to walk to the river just yet.

In a corner, was a small calabash of ground sorghum. Still aching, Hawecha squatted beside the hearth. Last night, there had been no time to light the fire, so there were no embers this morning. Ruefully, Hawecha realised that however badly she wished to hide today she would have to borrow a live coal from somebody.

Straightening up, she hobbled to the doorway and looked outside. The nearest hut was only a few paces away. She did not know the occupants. Well, there was nothing else to do but cross the empty space between them and introduce herself.

"I greet you, lady," she uttered timidly as she poked her head around the doorway, the words almost dying in her throat. "I ... I am Hawecha. New here since yesterday. I need ... I need a hot coal."

Bonsa looked up from her blazing fire and saw a beautiful yet frightened young woman standing before her. So this was the new addition to their village. This was Juldess' new bride. Poor girl! Bonsa had seen Juldess 'at work' on every young girl in turn, teasing and provoking them. Not a good character. Now that his father had chosen him a lovely woman, surely he would settle down?

"Come, my dear. Don't be afraid. I'm only old Bonsa. I shan't hurt you at all."

Her wrinkled face cracked into a smile of welcome and honesty. Hawecha looked into those rheumy old eyes and swore she saw some spark of mischief. The years had not bowed this woman's spirit. She returned the smile.

"Here's your coal. Now run along home, dear, and make breakfast for your husband. He's bound to appreciate that."

Hawecha did not dare confide in Bonsa that she didn't even know where Juldess was at this early hour. She was not sure if she was expected to cook his meal or not. She scuttled out, pretending to be extremely busy and hoped Bonsa would not notice the despair in her eyes.

Back inside her home, Hawecha burst into tears of anger, pain and frustration. Was this what married life was like? Not knowing where your husband was on the first morning of it? He had shamed her thoroughly.

The pangs of hunger still had to be dealt with. She had eaten nothing since her mother-in-law had made her coffee. A long, long time ago. She made a small pyramid of kindling (also thoughtfully provided for her) and blew upon Bonsa's coal. She would not need much of a fire, if this meal was for her alone. She poured water into a clay pot and set it on the fire to boil. Then added a handful of sorghum from the small calabash.

As she stirred the gruel with her three-pronged mixing stick, waiting for the porridge-like substance to thicken, she wondered what fate held in store for her. Marriage was supposed to be a sharing — to some extent. Men had their duties, which often took them away from the women for hours at a time. But the rest of the time, they shared life with their wives. Was Juldess that different from other men? It seemed she had made a very bad bargain.

Darmi appeared and offered to escort her down to the river. It was the same river of Hawecha' s childhood — just another part of it.

Hawecha hoped she would not break down with memories of long ago. She held her chin up, pretended all was well, and marched off beside her small companion, carrying the water-pot upon her head. As she strutted through the village, looking neither to left or right, the women noticed her proud carriage, the slimness of her neck, the small, straight shoulders, her small waist and the neat feet as one fell in front of the other; the daintiness of her step upon the ground, almost as though the earth made way for her. Ah yes, there walked a real beauty!

The river was wider here, though still the same shade of brown. There were many thorn-trees along its bank, providing welcome shade. A good place for the women to stop and gossip, as they collected water for the family or stripped completely to wash themselves all over. From earliest childhood, every Oromo was taught to keep clean — as clean as nature allowed for. Although she had already performed her ablutions in the privacy of her home, Hawecha longed to wash her troubles away in the broad, brown waters. Yet shyness prevented her from stripping here, amongst these strangers.

There were three women there before her, all cavorting happily in the river. This was the women's place and the women's hour: a brief respite from all their chores. They stretched out their time as long as they could, gossiping, teasing and chattering.

Hawecha did not know how to introduce herself. She hiked up her goatskin skirts about her waist, stepped ankle-deep into the river's edge, and slowly filled the water-pot.

"Who are you, girl?" a voice cried out, sharp and somewhat demanding. "We won't bite you. If you belong to our village, tell us who you are."

Hawecha looked up, the water-pot half filled. Emerging from the waters was a strongly built woman a little older than herself, taller than most women. Her breasts pointed upwards and outwards, yet the areola around the nipples were exceptionally black. So, high-breasted or not, Hawecha knew she had born one child at least.

"My name is Godanna-The-Strong and I want to be your friend. I will look after you."

Hawecha found it hard to resist such openness. Hesitantly, she gave her name and spoke of her recent marriage. The other women came up to listen. She was introduced to Dhaki-The-Story-Teller with pendulous breasts, flabby stomach and thighs that were creased and wrinkled. Her backside hung down 'to her knees' — as she herself cheerfully admitted.

The other woman, even younger than Hawecha, announced her name as Jataneh and explained that as yet, she had no noticeable role. She had been married for a year and, at last, a child was on its way. She pointed to her rounding belly.

So, here she was on her very first day with three friendly women in her life. A few more friends like this and Hawecha would survive, she supposed.

Yet, within minutes, as they walked back to the village, along the path, a quarrel broke out between Dhaki and Jataneh over a wooden bowl that the former had lent. It had been returned not properly cleaned. "So that's how it is," thought Hawecha. "Women are women the world over. I had better keep to myself."

When she got back to her home, her mother-in-law was waiting, in a state of agitation. "Where have you been, Hawecha?" she stormed. "My friends are waiting to meet you!"

Apologetically, Hawecha leaned the water-pot up against her own doorway and hurriedly followed Guyatu into her hut. Four women looked up as she appeared.

"A fine daughter-in-law you are," were the first words that accosted her. "How dare you treat Guyatu like this?" There followed an hour in which she was roundly scolded, reminded of her duties to her in-laws and thoroughly put down.

Hawecha at last was permitted to return to her own hut, as subdued as if she had been physically whipped. Once more, she was overwhelmed by tears. She swept the floor and tidied up the pile of goatskins upon the bed. She washed her utensils carefully, throwing the waste water just to the left of her own doorway. The remainder of the day passed in quiet, woman's work.

Juldess appeared at sunset, sat down upon his stool and demanded water. She stepped over the large log upon the ground that separated the public area of the hut from the private sleeping quarters. Obediently, she served him.

Then he asked for food. No conversation, no explanation of where he had been. "Out," was his brief response to her carefully-phrased questioning.

Blowing upon the embers of her morning's fire, she added a little kindling and then placed her clay cooking pot upon the hearth. Repeating her actions of the morning, she poured in water and waited for it to boil. She emptied the sorghum from the calabash and with her mixing stick in her left hand, stirred the mixture slowly. Her right hand was at her throat, fingering her protective amulet. "God keep me calm." She prayed. Cooking food was a holy occupation, to be approached with care and respect. The hearth-stones formed the very foundation of family life. Every woman was supposed to purify herself somehow before she fed her household.

She heard a soft, calm voice inside her head: Suleh, her beloved friend. "Don't be afraid of your anger, Hawecha. It is justified. But don't put it into the food. Do as your mother did in times like these. Pray for peace to come."

*"God, give me strength to bear this man.*
*Give my thoughts good grace.*
*Give me something else to think of than my anger.*
*Fill my heart with thoughts of peace."*

Feeling greatly soothed, Hawecha continued to stir. In the evening, the porridge was always thicker than the thin gruel of the morning. "To sit on the stomach at night," as they said. Every now and then, Hawecha twirled her mixing-stick between her two palms, so there would be no lumps in the mixture. Her mother and aunt had taught her well.

Except for the rare occasions on which they ate meat, sorghum would provide their daily sustenance. Milk was reserved for children, nursing mothers and the elderly. Coffee was for rituals, or for visitors and friends. Hawecha wondered how many times she would prepare a potful of gruel in this same time-honoured way. Thousands, she supposed.

They ate in silence. That night, Juldess hurled himself upon her twice. She responded as best she could. Again, in the morning, he had gone. Hawecha did not dare complain to his mother. She thought of old Bonsa, who had seemed so genuinely friendly. After all, she had borrowed a hot coal. Perhaps she could give something in return?

She cast her eyes upon her few possessions. She could not part with her containers, nor any of her cooking utensils. The digging sticks were vital and so were all the goatskins. She raised her eyes to the upper levels of the hut. There, from a small twig she had stuck into the woven outer structure of the walls, hung a string of iron beads that had belonged to her grandmother, Ayo Midadu, the Beauty. Surely, her mother would be angry if she parted with such a heritage?

Well, she would just have to take herself and ask Bonsa if she needed help. A good excuse for getting some practical advice.

"You may sweep for me," Bonsa announced. "These old bones grow older every minute." The old woman sat outside, well out of the way of the flying dust.

When Hawecha had finished the task, she decided to broach the painful subject of her marriage. Falteringly, she explained her problem. "He ... he is just never there," she quavered. "I've only prepared one meal for him in two whole days," she moaned. "What am I doing wrong?"

Bonsa probed into the matter of married life. Was Hawecha pleasant? Did she accept her husband's advances? Had they in fact consummated the marriage properly? Was Hawecha responding with passion?

Hawecha — in deep embarrassment — described the ache between her legs, the blood upon her thighs and the way in which Juldess had thrust himself upon her so fiercely, five times altogether.

The old woman sighed. She had counselled so many young women in her long, long life. So many problems she had heard. Some were mendable and some not. She knew that Juldess liked women — having observed him with her shrewd eyes on many occasions. Now Hawecha had spoken of his ardour. Bonsa understood that it was not Hawecha that Juldess wanted. Any woman would do. Yes, there were men like that. Men who took and used. She sighed in pity for this young wife.

"Juldess is a trader's son, you must remember," she explained. "Traders are not like ordinary people. They come and go and the wind itself cannot hold them. He must keep his business going. You just come to me when things go wrong, or when you need somebody to talk to."

She patted Hawecha's hand, the young one lying passive beneath the hand that had lived ... for oh, so many years now!

As Hawecha left, looking fairly composed, Bonsa wondered what the future would bring. Children, she hoped. Bonsa had brought many into this world and was by now renowned for her skills as a midwife. She knew herbs that would keep the mother calm in labour and she knew of one leaf that, when boiled, made a decoction to deaden the pain of menstrual cramps. Ah yes, if she had time to make her preparations, she could deal with most of women's ailments. Alas, there was not always time!

She covertly studied Hawecha. Slim and strong and not too narrow about the pelvis. But perhaps not much will — and often it was will that birthed a baby. She would have to keep an eye on Hawecha. That was all. And as for her marital problems, well, many women made do with the love of their children.

Meanwhile, Hawecha needed more sorghum. She walked out through the outer enclosure of the village, to the fields beyond. She could hear women singing as they harvested. With the sharp knife she had tucked into her waist, she cut off seven tall stalks; for 'one-and-a-half of us,' she thought, these would be sufficient. She returned and stacked them inside the small granary to the right of her own doorway.

In the afternoon, she spent her time in rolling threads of wild fibre across her thigh to twist them into a new thong. One of her sandals needed mending. She had noticed that the ground beneath the trees along the river bank was very thorny in places. Presumably, she would wear sandals more often here.

Later in the day, as she sat inside musing upon the ancient land of Fugug, a bright blue butterfly fluttered in and circled over her head before it found its way out once more into the sunshine: an excellent omen. Surely she would find happiness one day! Perhaps life was not so terrible after all? Better an absent husband than one who shouted at her.

Furthermore, she was not at the very bottom of the village hierarchy. Children and young girls all had to obey her. Yes, they had to respect her. Hawecha brightened up considerably and smiled at all the world.

# CHAPTER 14

For the fifth month in a row, her leather breech-clout showed signs of blood. Despite all Juldess efforts, Hawecha was still not pregnant. "Shame on you! Despite your high ways, you bring shame!" Juldess stormed out of the hut, leaving her to weep.

Marriage had not softened him, nor made him change his ways. He either spoke not at all, or ordered her about peremptorily. He came and went — mostly went — so she hardly ever saw him during the day. He would throw a full goatskin of coffee-beans upon the floor of the hut, as a sign of clever trading and assume that was the end of his responsibilities to her. That, and begetting children.

Outside the hut, however, Hawecha gained in popularity. She made a point of greeting everybody morning, noon and night in the proper manner. It was a long, polite greeting. She never missed a word of it.

Every day, when her own chores were done with, she asked her mother-in-law what she could do to assist her. There were always several 'somethings' on Guyatu's list: pounding grain in a hollowed out wooden container with a hefty pole; sweeping out the hut; helping with visitors, of whom there were many; holding babies while their mothers rested; or mending this and that. Sometimes, Guyatu would send a small child with a message that she should help with the milking the following morning.

The family, as has been said, was wealthy. Apart from six horses, they owned forty or so goats and roughly one hundred cattle. The livestock was husbanded carefully. It represented a trade item, future bride-price, gifts for ceremonies and from time to time was eaten in times of drought. A wise stock-holder managed his herds with skill, hoping for endless increase. Whilst Juldess had taken on most of the trading, his father and uncle were responsible for the welfare of the livestock. But men never did the milking.

There was always the incessant problem of grazing. In times of plenty, the herds pastured around the village. But when the dry season came, the men often took them off great distances. Only a small nucleus herd was left behind, to sustain the remainder of the family. The men would remain away for weeks on end, until rain made it safe for them to return.

Guyatu had one sister who helped her — a morose widow named Darmi-The-Pout. But if the herds increased, as they did in times of plenty, an extra pair of hands was vital.

Soon, the milking became an almost daily event. Hawecha came to love the smell and feel of goats. She listened to their endless bleatings and imagined their conversations: probably about Godanna-The-Strong or Hawecha-The-Weak. When a new kid was born, she would hold it to her breast and bless it. She would watch its first hesitant steps or the first time it suckled.

Often, Hawecha would be left in charge of the goats. She would take them out through the enclosure and find a patch of grazing away from other herds. Then she would "hah!" and "shoo!" them into obedience and guide them with her stick. In the morning, they would have to be driven to the river and in the evening, they had to be guided back into the corral.

Gradually, Guyatu began to realise she had acquired a pearl of a daughter-in-law and treated Hawecha more kindly. Other newly-weds and younger women joined her at the river. Whilst men traded in livestock, the women traded in gossip. Hawecha laughed now, sometimes, having lost her initial reserve. She felt she'd been accepted. Older women liked her and admired for being a hard worker and for putting up with a difficult situation. Word had spread that Juldess was not very kind to her.

Hawecha managed to fill her days. Her spiritual life had been set aside for now. She was often simply too tired to think of stars or old stories. Once in a while, Suleh spoke usually advising her to keep calm, or to rest when she could. Clearly, Suleh could not change Hawecha's life. Her visits were just acts of friendship.

Eight months after the consummation of her marriage, her breech-clout was free from blood. Hawecha waited. Nothing. At last, Juldess would be happy! He had gone to a far-off settlement for many days, to intercept a Somali horse caravan. The village needed salt and spices urgently. The Somali travelled in the north and east and even to the Horn of Africa, where they met Indians and Arabs. Ah well, a few more days or weeks and she could tell him.

He returned puffed up with success and made straight for his father. "I sold sixteen goats and bought a heap of useful goods." The men unloaded his two horses and four donkeys. The women came out to watch the process. Much wealth lay there.

They began to haggle. "Three eggs in exchange for the red beads, Juldess" or "I'd like some of those spices you brought last time. They made my old goat meat so tasty! I give this calabash in exchange." On and on the bartering continued, interspersed by arguments and shrillness. Even the old men lost their supposedly aloof demeanour.

Within two hours, half the merchandise had been disposed of and a pile of payments lay beside Juldess. Hawecha stepped forward to help carry the goods into the hut.

Soon, it resembled a store-house: goatskins filled with grain, to supplement their own supplies; bags of coriander, cloves, and cumin; dried chilli peppers – a great rarity; leather thongs; and even thick ropes for leading camels, although, so far, they had none. The salt she laid by was sufficient to last the entire village three months. Nearby he placed a bagful of gaudy glass bangles. "Made in India," Juldess explained as she eyed them covetously. "Not for you. These are for business!" Her euphoria evaporated immediately.

When all was carefully counted and put away, Hawecha decided to tell him her good news.

"Is it mine?"

Hawecha stood there open-mouthed. How did he dare to accuse her of infidelity? And with whom? She held her marriage vows sacred. One man was enough for her. To look for another was not only trouble, but totally beyond her capacity.

He pushed her down onto the bed and forced himself upon her. "Just to show you who is boss here!" then he stormed out to brag and swagger before the men-folk.

After a time, the baby quickened and Hawecha's belly began to swell. Old Bonsa noticed and was delighted. Yet there were deep grey shadows beneath Hawecha's eyes, and the girl looked a bit thinner than before. Something was much amiss. Bonsa decided to talk it over with Guyatu.

"I'm worried," Bonsa announced without preamble. "This daughter-in-law of yours gives me trouble. I don't like the look of things. Is Juldess beating her?"

Only an old midwife like Bonsa would have dared to ask such a question. Guyatu flew into a violent temper, shouting, gesticulating, spitting on the ground and only just drawing short of putting a curse upon her. In the end, Bonsa withdrew. With *that* family as his background, she wouldn't be surprised if Juldess *did* beat his new wife every single day.

She determined to ask Hawecha who hung her head and denied it. "Only once. He ... he pushed me onto the floor."

There came a day when Hawecha felt a pain deep in her very being. She knew at once what it augured. Time for the baby to come. Within a few minutes, the pain was followed by another. It was too early for the baby, surely? She crossed over to Bonsa's and explained what was happening.

Bonsa had been prepared and at once made a pain-killing decoction. She made Hawecha drink it. Hawecha was escorted back to her own home. When the contractions increased in severity, Godanna was called to hold Hawecha's back while Darmi was sent off to fetch more water. The women gathered in time-old tradition, to assist at this new birth.

Bonsa made Hawecha squat down over a hide laid upon the floor. As the pains grew in intensity, they gave her a thick stick to bite on and in between the labour pains, they marched her up and down.

Alas, their efforts were in vain. When at long last the girlchild made an appearance, it was stillborn. The women removed the evidence of birth and after–birth and buried everything well outside the settlement. Bonsa took from around her neck a cowrie shell on a thong and placed it around Hawecha's, to ward off further evil. Then she commanded prayers for the release of the infant's soul.

Hawecha wept as though her heart would break in half. As a mother, she had failed completely.

Bonsa gave her a calming potion and to it added a herbal soporific. Hawecha slept on and off for two days. Her recovery was slow. When she walked for the first time down to the river for water, Godanna had to help her.

Juldess made himself scarce. Bonsa could not persuade him that he had in any way been responsible. Guyatu, who had grown jealous of the role Hawecha had played in her son's life, now mourned for the grandchild she could not have. Would never have, according to Bonsa, who had firmly declared that Hawecha would bear no more children. Juldess had torn something inside Hawecha's womb, with his violence. Guyatu saw Juldess with open eyes at last. Yet even she could not get him to agree that he was at least partly to blame.

Time passed, and Hawecha healed in her body. Her soul was another matter. The brief sight of that tiny body — a girl, a piece of herself — had completely unnerved her. She became listless and sad. The hut was a little untidy now and there were often lumps in her gruel.

"Give it time," the women said.

Meanwhile, Juldess came and went more so than before. "Trouble!" the women gossiped far and wide about the marriage.

One day, as Hawecha came back from the fields alone, carrying her allotment of sorghum stalks, she heard a giggle behind a thick bush. A shadowy form danced away.

Three weeks later, Godanna developed a large bruise on one arm. She claimed she had bumped into her own doorpost, but everyone knew Godanna only bumped into the things she wanted to bump into.

Shortly thereafter, Hawecha decided to make a longer walk to the well of Great Thirst. They only used this if the river shrank too much, or if the river-water became too muddied by the hoofs of cattle. The well was extremely deep. Dug long ago by their forebears, it took seven men to reach down and pass the leather buckets of water up to men at the top.

Sometimes Gabbra camel owners passed this way: Gabbra with their harsher voices and more guttural tongue. Their gesticulations were more marked; the jewellery of their women slightly different. The camels themselves were a marvel, with their immense height. Hawecha admired their enormous flared nostrils, vast teeth, slobbering jaws and knock-knees. She did not admire their flatulence, however, nor their great deposits of dung. Nonetheless, it was always good to see a different side of life. Perhaps the longer walk would cheer her up?

Alas, no camels that day! Disconsolately, she retraced her steps. She paused to turn towards a cluster of trees, much in need of shade. As she approached, she espied two figures; one male and one female. The man held the woman by both arms. They were gazing into each other's eyes. The woman's shoulder-wrap lay on the ground. She looked at those proud breasts. Juldess and Godanna!

Ashamed to her very roots, Hawecha turned around and ran. Ran until her chest heaved with the unaccustomed exertion. Gasping for breath, she threw herself upon her bed. The sobs came from deep inside her belly.

From within her shame, there ultimately rose a great rage. A determination to rule her own life now. Had she not bowed down before her uncle's will, in order to be married? Never, never would she share this bed again. Juldess had shamed her into rebellion. Hawecha was a Chosen One and now she would exert herself. She decided to make a formal complaint against Juldess and press her case before Jarso.

# CHAPTER 15

In the morning, the news was all over the village. Juldess had disappeared  and so had Godanna, whom they now christened the Faithless One. The worst of it was that she had left behind her two growing boys. What kind of mother would ever leave her children? Their father was shattered. He announced that he felt unable to care for them. It was left to their old grandmother to take them in.

Hawecha decided she would visit her aunt and uncle, in the hope that the furore would die down. She borrowed a donkey from her in-laws, who supported her in her decision. Their son was henceforth outcast from his parents' home. As far as they were concerned, the High Priests would determine the future.

For the first time since her marriage she made the journey home — for "home" it had remained. News had come to her from time to time of new births of twins, and of the death of a warrior in a distant battle. Her old friend Choleh had produced a second daughter. She hoped the friendship would still hold for them both. Hawecha badly needed a friend.

She left at sunrise, with her in-laws' blessings, bearing gifts of salt, beads and tobacco for her aunt and uncle.

How much more pleasant this ride was than the one that had taken her away from her original village. How much more comfortable she felt sitting upon a broad-backed donkey than upon that nervy horse. And how agreeable to be low off the ground, rather than up at a great height. Even with all her miseries, she found herself enjoying these comparisons.

The village looked much as it had when she left it ... how long ago now? Almost a year and a half? She saw three more houses within the enclosure and it looked as though the ritual hut had been rebuilt.

She assumed that everybody had heard her latest news. Protocol demanded that she speak to the highest authority in the village. Buleh-The-Ritual-Leader or her uncle, the councillor? She decided that her uncle most probably took precedence. His job took him far and wide, whereas Buleh's role was only a local one.

She dismounted outside the thorn enclosure. A woman came to see who it was. She clapped her hands when she recognized Hawecha. "My dear, I have longed to see you again!" It was Wareh, her older adoptive sister. "Oh, so sorry about your little baby; poor you!" she added, giving her a great hug.

Chuquliss, it transpired, was at work in the fields still. Wareh began asking questions. Hawecha decided not to divulge any details of her present predicament. Time enough for that. She greeted Wareh in a most friendly manner, then made her excuses, saying she had something urgent to deliver to Jarso.

Taking her small bundle of gifts, she made straight for his hut. Galgalu had aged somewhat and complained of some innards trouble. She made Hawecha sit down after her long ride and probed for news.

"Not without my uncle," was Hawecha's firm reply, not knowing from where she drew such strength. Inside, all she wanted was another good cry and to feel her aunt's arms wrapped round her and soothing words poured into her two ears. Oh, to be like a small child again. Instead, she put a brave face on it and spoke of this and that.

It seemed old Jarso was at that moment sitting beneath the elders' tree with other elders. The Oromo lived by the complicated age-set system called *gada*. Every eight years, a major ceremony was held during which elders could retire from political office. They undertook to guide and counsel their juniors who assumed power in their place. This ceremony was called *gadamoji*. Half way in between the *gadamoji* ceremonies, another ceremony took place. It was a gathering of law-makers and was held at a place called Gaayo. Laws and decisions made during this gathering could not be overturned by any other Oromo.

Galgalu explained that the gathering of law-makers was now being organised. Jarso, as a respected councillor, had to be present during the meetings, which might last for several weeks. He was talking to Harero-The-Spiritual-Leader and to two venerable and aged elders whom he hoped would accompany him on the journey.

Hawecha sighed. Her uncle would be detained for hours yet. What could she do to stop her aunt from uncovering the reason for her presence? She decided to feign fatigue and request a long nap. "Please awaken me when he returns, aunt." She had of course heard of Hawecha's stillbirth and also rumours of Juldess's philandering. The poor girl appeared exhausted. Well, she would wait, then.

It was very late in the afternoon when Jarso returned. Hawecha woke up at the sound of his voice. He was full of grumbles. The two elders had refused to go with him to the meeting, claiming that the journey would kill them both, since they were both over eighty. Hawecha felt their refusal was utterly justified. After all, it meant at least two weeks without the comforts of home. Hawecha felt that at times, her uncle was stubborn as a donkey.

As for Harero, although he had been greatly flattered, he had trodden on a sharp stick a few days before and the open wound in his foot had begun to fester. It was painfully evident that he could not undertake a long trip — however holy in intention it might be.

Finally, Galgalu succeeded in calming him down. "You will just have to go alone then. You are well known and you have many friends along the way. You cannot possibly get lost; you've been there twice before now."

Having rid himself of all his personal problems, he at last took notice of the fact that Hawecha was actually *there.*

"My dear girl, have you come to visit us? Good, you will keep Galgalu out of mischief while I'm gone."

He was on the point of sweeping out of the house again, when Hawecha blocked his passage. "Uncle, I am not here for fun," she announced soberly. "I am here to *stay!*"

"You ... you *what!*" he thundered.

Hawecha explained as best she could between a thousand interruptions and ejaculations from Jarso and an equal number of "God, protect us!" from poor Galgalu. Both of them were stunned.

Old Jarso stroked his short greying beard. Here was a problem indeed! For a married woman to leave her husband was unthinkable and unheard of. "But, uncle, *he* left *me.*" Hawecha had to remind him.

He lowered his head into his hands, bowed down with the shame and the pain of it. What was he to do? Not only had Juldess left Hawecha he had taken another man's wife away with him. So, two marriages were accursed now. He rocked back and forth on his stool, groaning with the sheer impossibility of the situation. Divorce was a rare event in Oromo culture.

"Were you nice to him?" he fired at Hawecha.

"Oh, uncle! You brought me up to be good and dutiful. I did my duty, even though it hurt more than a little. In fact, the first night it hurt a lot!" Unable to take any more brow beating, Hawecha's shoulders heaved with sobs.

Jarso realised she had reached the limits of endurance. Instead of the comfortable life he had tried to give her, it seemed he had cast her to a demon.

"There, there, my child. Your mother was a good woman and I brought you up to be like her." Seeing Galgalu about to fly at him for forgetting her part in her niece's upbringing, he hastily added: "and of course your aunt did too. We both did our very best."

Somewhat mollified and seeing that he was perhaps able to take her part in this dreadful matter after all, Hawecha timidly reminded him that Suleh had lived without a husband in the end and had become their beloved teacher.

"I dream of Suleh sometimes and remember, if you please, that I warned you all of the famine. You didn't listen to me. Look what happened! Everyone knows I am a Chosen One. I know I'm still young, but Juldess has left me. Do you want me to call him back? Where from?"

Then she suggested that he take the matter with him and present it before the Council. It was like holding a hot coal to the kindling.

"What!" he roared. "The Council has far larger issues with which to occupy its time than a broken marriage."

Galgalu reminded him that there were two.

"Women, women, trouble-making women!"

Hawecha interjected, with a calm that came from she knew not where. "This time it is a man who has undone our people. Be fair. I speak the truth." She drew herself up as high and as haughty as she could.

Jarso realised that she was a child no longer. Whatever marriage had done to her, she had returned an adult and one with a mind of her own.

"The problem is too big for you, uncle. If you take it to the Council, it will become their problem. They will discuss it and come to a wise decision."

"Whence came her wisdom?" Jarso wondered. He realised she had given him a way out. Yet male pride prevented him from acquiescing immediately.

He paced up and down. Back and forth he trod, hopping inelegantly over the log that separated hearth from bedroom, fingering his beard, wringing his hands and calling upon the spirit of the great sage and mystic Sofmari to come to his aid. Finally, when he could milk the situation no longer, he announced: "I will sleep on this. I will tell you my decision in the morning."

And with that, the women had to content themselves.

# CHAPTER 16

Hawecha barely slept that night and who could wonder at this? Her life had been thrown into ruin by her husband's foolishness. Where did she stand now, in tribal structure? Women had no age-set. They adopted that of their husbands. Nor had she any useful role at present. Not a wife and not a mother. Not a daughter even. She tossed and turned, with dark thoughts spinning in her head.

Long before cock-crow, she was up, muzzy with exhaustion. She stretched herself and tiptoed silently through the hut and out into fresh air.

The sun was barely rising, caught at the horizon's very edge in a web of soft gold. She watched, as within minutes the orb rose a little higher; bathed in crimson and pink. Small clouds of a darker pink hue were scattered across the sky in horizontal layers. It was a glorious beginning to the day.

How could she remain sad, in the face of a great dawn such as this one? Hawecha decided to be grateful for these wonders. She would deal with her despair and fear by occupying herself with hard work.

In three days, Jarso was due to depart. There were many days – if not weeks – ahead of her, before he returned to them with news of the wise ones' decision. That decision would alter the course of her life, she knew. Why was life not hers to make? Why did men-folk rule over everything? Not everything. She recalled Suleh had ruled over women in her days. So had her own grandmother. There were a few precedents in their oral tradition for women like her.

But what was she, then? Untried and untested. She had received one warning from an external source which her uncle had refused to take seriously. She did not herself make prophecies, nor was she yet one of their rare mystics. She could not throw sandals to divine the future; she was not a famous reader of entrails. Indeed, she had never witnessed one at work. She was not an expert who studied the stars, reckoned time and announced the days of special prayers. Hawecha realised that, in fact, she wasn't anything much. A young woman, formerly married and without a husband; she had no status. Why was the world so unfair?

Jarso meanwhile, had also passed a sleepless night, tossing and turning until poor Galgalu had asked him to lie under the stars or else she would. Being the woman, it was she who in the end stalked out cursing and grumbling into the dark night, dragging a goatskin with her as a covering.

Now, he arose, with the decision clear in his mind. Before Galgalu had even lit the fire, as every good housewife must, he made a great pronouncement. He would go to Gaayo as planned, but he would not go there alone. Hawecha would have to accompany him. She would stand there in the Court of Law and speak for herself. After all, he was learning her story second-hand and she was the very best witness. If she could sway the other councillors ... if she could persuade them to annul her marriage; it would all be up to her.

And so it came to pass that, three days later, Hawecha once more sat upon a small and brave donkey, plodding along behind her uncle. He remained aloof and far ahead of her, as though he were dragging her to the meeting. What had she done? What did men want? Were all women so abused?

They stopped only to sip water from their goatskins, or to relieve themselves behind a convenient bush. At night, they stopped in a village, ate hurriedly, slept and then pushed on. Jarso buried himself in a cloud of self-importance, making it quite clear that he was on a quest of sorts and had no time to discuss trivia and frivolities with lesser mortals. He put everyone off with his abruptness.

"Ay, what a hard man!" Hawecha heard one hostess remark to a neighbour. "What a fool he is, to be sure. So unbending and unfriendly. He will come this way again one day. What sort of greeting does he think we will give him next time?"

Jarso was leaving a trail of unpopularity behind him and Hawecha felt pity for him. In his heart of hearts, he was not a bad man. But his role had made him rather pompous as he grew older and by now, he would brook no opposition. What kind of councillor is he, Hawecha wondered? Once he had been deemed wise. Perhaps in the company of his peers he became more respectful and allowed others equal say. Well, in due course, she would see him in action for herself.

The scenery changed a little on the third day. More hilly and less thorny. Overhead, the clouds were still small puffballs of white, floating in a pale blue vastness. They might even be the same clouds from her village following her to her fate, Hawecha mused. Much good they would do her, since they neither spoke nor pointed the way ahead. She had always loved the clouds, yet now, she almost came to hate them.

On the fifth day, the rumours caught up with them. The news of Juldess' disappearance had given rise to endless gossip and speculation, which rapidly travelled from one end of Liban to another and even into land belonging to the Konso people, to the west.

In time it reached the Somali people of the east. The rumours flew, the facts were embroidered upon. As if they needed any embroidery. In themselves, they were quite shocking! Had he gone with Godanna to her parents' village? Absolutely not. They would not let the miserable couple in. No, they would have to leave the Oromo completely. Were they with the Gabbra then? This was quite possible. Until they all remembered that Godanna liked her creature comforts and absolutely hated camels. Had they fled to join a caravan of Somali traders? This eventuality seemed by far the most likely. They would have to convert to Islam, of course, but neither Juldess nor Godanna were particularly noted for the fervour of their prayers.

Hawecha could picture Godanna amongst the beautiful Somali women. She would hold her own there. She would buy brilliantly coloured silks with wide patterned borders, and walk about veiled, as their rich women did.

Juldess had taken all of his six horses with him. With them and his reputation as a trader, he would do extremely well. Godanna would join the ranks of the wealthy. She would smile and pout and perhaps even flirt with other men, twisting them round her little finger. She would sway seductively, or stand there with her hands on her hips, making her breasts jut out even further.

Far from envying her, Hawecha rejoiced at her own sudden freedom. How strange that Juldess was always after this ephemeral and fleeting thing and yet, *she,* Hawecha, had won it. This thought gave her deep satisfaction and kept her company as they meandered onwards.

They were heading south-eastwards to the accustomed site for the meeting. This was an ancient well. Ahead — at last — could be seen tracts of acacia woodland, promising welcome shade and rest. They plodded further along the track made wide by the passage of thousands of feet and thousands of cattle, goats and donkeys over the many years of usage. Soon, they saw the law-makers' temporary settlement, within the usual thorn bush enclosure. Inside the periphery were small corrals for horses, cattle, goats and camels.

In the centre of the enclosure, forming a large curve, were the huts… twenty or so… somewhat hastily put together. At one end lived the "president" of the assembly. Jarso dismounted and signalled for Hawecha to do likewise.

"I must pay my respects."

He tethered his donkey to one of three trees within the compound, and marched off. "Come!" he called to Hawecha over his shoulder. Hawecha stumbled after him, hoping her skirts and shoulder wrap were in order. She lost a sandal and had to hop about until she had found it again. She wiped her sweating hands on her long skirts and straightened her back.

"Stay there."

Jarso swept into the hut as Hawecha stood outside, awaiting further instructions.

# CHAPTER 17

Hawecha looked about. Never before had she seen such a large gathering of people! Surely a hundred lived here now? She imagined each hut with its elder and its housewife, a relative or two and who knew how many children? Three boys were crouched in the shade playing with their clay animals. She watched as the boys made the little bulls mount the even smaller cows.

She thought of Juldess treatment towards her. All that love she had felt for him when he had come to the village as her chosen bridegroom, bringing the bride-price with him. He had behaved like an animal with her, just like a bull.

Such thoughts were useless now. Love had gone. She turned her mind back to studying the settlement. She knew the huts were constructed in order of seniority. Since she stood outside the house of the "president", she could safely assume that next door lived a councillor or clan leader. To her left, the huts would be occupied by families in descending order of precedence, according to their ancient protocol.

Would nobody offer her a drink of water? Where were all the women? They were probably collecting firewood, gossiping at the well, or enjoying the shade of their huts. She herself was feeling more than a little hot as the merciless sun moved higher in its own arc from east to west.

As if sensing her predicament, a little girl, a tiny mite of maybe four or five, trundled up to her on chubby feet and held out a small wooden cup full of water. Lispingly, she announced that her mother had ordered Hawecha to sit down.

Hawecha slid her back down the doorpost and gratefully sank to her haunches. Then, she stuck her legs straight out in front and felt the support of the post behind her. How good it was! She thanked the child, returned the empty cup and sank into a semi-doze.

"Hey, you!" a rough male voice aroused her. "They are waiting for you inside; come at once. Come girl, the Father wishes to see you." A tall, spare man with only one eye towered over her. The lid of the other eye was closed over the concave hollow behind it. "What had gouged it out," she wondered. "Was it a fierce and bloody battle?" It took a few moments for her own eyes to adjust to the inner darkness.

"Well girl, start from the beginning."

She could barely make out the form of an old man sitting upon his stool. Gradually, she noticed his head was completely shaven, meaning he had gone through his *gadamoji* ceremony.

Such men were deemed to be closer to God than anyone else, apart from the five High Priests. Not every elder became a *gadamoji*. It was a matter of individual choice, thus one who had put away all thoughts of power and leadership was held in the highest esteem. Hawecha assumed he would be fair with her and listen to her story carefully, without prejudgement.

Custom forbade her to sit before this sage. Straightening her spine, she began, faltering badly, mixing up the order of events and repeating herself frequently, until she grew more confident. The old man only interrupted her once. "Repeat that for me." And once more she told of her very-near-rape.

At last, the miserable tale was told and she hung her head in embarrassment. It had been a difficult matter to divulge.

"We will discuss this, we the elders. It is an uncommon tale. We must make a wise judgement, lest it be held against us later on. I will call the other *gadamoji* to pray with me first. We must know and understand and implement the wishes of the Great Creator. It will take time."

He instructed Hawecha and Jarso to leave him. Separate accommodation would be arranged for them within the compound. He ordered his son — himself a man of perhaps fifty years of age — to find homes for them. "Treat them well. They have come far."

Hawecha blessed him for his kindness.

She was introduced to a woman who was surly and overworked. Four small children undoubtedly accounted for this. With all the meals that had to be prepared, she was glad of Hawecha's helping hands. She showed her around and explained which pot stood where, pointed to the guest bed and left. Hawecha became used to her comings and goings at short notice. It seemed the poor woman had a serious bladder problem.

For three days, she saw nothing of her uncle. Nor was she called again before the Father of this assembly. The womenfolk, however, knew exactly what was going on. "They are dealing with the matter of a bride-price which has not yet been produced." She was informed.

The next day it would be the problem of a prize bull over which two men were arguing. Willing buyer and unwilling seller. The former said the latter had gone back upon his word — unthinkable behaviour!

From the main entrance to the compound, a broad track ran through the woodlands. "Where does it lead?" she asked one of the younger married women who had befriended her. "All the way to Mega," Zugura replied.

"Is it far from us?" Hawecha queried.

"No, only three days if you ride upon a donkey. Faster on a horse or camel, naturally."

Hawecha's face broke into a wide grin, a demonstration of her inner joy. Mega was one of the great places she had dreamed of visiting. So, here she was in her twentieth year and already she stood near to it. Who knew? The next day, she might actually be sent there.

Reality brought her down to earth abruptly, however. On the third day, a young man came to fetch her. The message was brief. "Come at once. You must present your case!"

The elders were gathered under a wide-spreading thorn tree. What a throng! She could smell the body-heat as they all sat there on the ground, huddled close together in order not to miss a single important word. Being old men, some of them smelled not of rancid sweat but of inner bodily disorders.

Different faces graced the occasion; some lined with wisdom hard-won; some with shrewd and manipulative eyes; others calm and noble in appearance; yet there were others with hooded eyes, shielding their thoughts. All these men had power, of one sort or another. Each showed his rank or special office by the wearing of an armlet, or by the holding of a special stick. Amongst them sat several *gadamoji*. Directly beneath the shade tree, the 'president' sat upon the sacred stool, used since time immemorial. In front of him was a small clearing.

"Where is the plaintiff Hawecha?"

Two men pushed her forwards.

# CHAPTER 18

Two raucous crows chose that moment to land in the higher branches of the tree. This gave rise to much whispering. Not a good omen. There was a foreboding, much argument and even shouting. Her case had begun badly.

The elders decided to pray, even though a full day of prayer had preceded the opening of the Assembly.

There were no women present. Hawecha fumed as she stood there waiting for the signal to begin. Her uncle sat to one side of the Father, she noticed. He had reached the highest rank, then. Or was it just because of her? Why were women not allowed here? Why were they not councillors? They gave birth to children and raised them. Yet, they had no real authority.

At last the 'president' spoke. "Repeat what you have told me and do not be afraid to do so."

"I ... I prefer to speak before women. Or at least one woman. May I not have a kindred spirit present?" What presumption. Yet nobody dared to speak.

The Father of the Assembly was seen to murmur unto himself, his lips forming the words of a private prayer. A long pause ensued.

"Call my wife. Let her come before us and stand next to Hawecha. The girl has undergone enough torture. She is within her rights."

Hawecha trembled violently and sought to fight back the tears of relief that overwhelmed her. This was no place for crying like a small child. She had to prove herself as a woman.

Gatto was brought forward. She stood beside Hawecha, thin and proud. Never had she stood in front of her own husband this way. The men would decide the outcome, but if they asked for her opinion, she would speak up without fear. She would support Hawecha's side of the story against anything a man could venture to say.

Gatto was known to be a silent woman, one who spoke only when she felt she had something worth saying. The Father had chosen this female representative well. He had laid his own relationship to her to one side, showing his tolerance and objectivity. Nobody doubted his wisdom.

Now he signalled for Hawecha to speak. She turned towards the old lady and directed the facts to her. All the utter humiliation of it. All the months of suffering she had endured. The beating, the death of her baby and her inability to have another one. How she had seen her own husband clutch at another woman. How that woman had won, against all justice. "Stolen, mind you. She 'stole' my husband from me!" Greatly emboldened — and surprised at the vehemence of her feelings — she now turned towards the men.

"I urge you to judge them harshly. Before you lies a broken heart that was young once, now grown old and weary with grief."

As she finished, she collapsed into Gatto's arms. Now she had told the truth before the whole world. Now, at last, she could cry.

Old Gatto stroked her hair and shoulders and murmured soothing words into Hawecha's ears. "Be calm, my girl. You have spoken with admirable courage. Never has a woman's point of view been so well expressed. My husband is a great man. Some of them are, you know. Be calm now. It is important."

At last, Hawecha became herself again.

"Forgive me my Fathers and Elders. Forgive a young one for her unseemly tears."

The old man arose from his sacred stool and pounded on the ground with the stick that had once belonged to his great grandfather, of holy name and holy repose, as all deceased leaders should be. "Order! Let us come to order!" he shouted.

"The elders and I must retire from this Assembly and pray yet again for collective wisdom. I have arranged this astonishing case to be the last item on our long and difficult agenda. We will now withdraw. Meanwhile, I ask you all, both male and female to add your prayers to ours."

The crowd made way as the solemn procession of leaders left them. They would gather together in small groups. They would pray for wisdom. Gatto headed towards her own home.

Hawecha announced that she wished to be alone for a while and made for the open bushland beyond the tall trees. She wandered through the bushes, avoiding the thorns that scratched her arms and legs and always threatened to detain one. She was in a daze. Had she really spoken up in front of the leaders? Had they truly brought forward a woman to give her strength? It was almost like a dream — not quite believable. And yet, it had happened. Would it become a part of oral history, this strange story of hers? Would the great storytellers embellish the facts with their skill and mastery of timing and of words? Above all, she wondered what the outcome would be and whether the story-tellers would tell the truth, or invent a better ending.

She came to a small open area. There stood an ancient grave. Unknown hands had made a great pile of black rocks here and surrounded it with a wall of shiny white stones. A great ancestor lay here — perhaps a former spiritual leader who still listened to difficult cases. Hawecha sat down beside the grave, to follow this train of thought.

She realised that — despite her anger against the way in which men ruled the lives of all — there was much goodness in the tribal laws. The age-set system ensured that each man grew up slowly and could never over-reach himself. From baby to early childhood he grew, that growth noticed only once every eight years. As a young man, he moved into his period of warriorhood fighting to protect the cattle, or the women. He might even die protecting his people: surely, a noble ending?

The Oromo believed in collective responsibility, which outlasted a man's lifespan. All that their forebears had done, suffered, or not done, rested upon them.

Once a man had become a *gadaa,* meaning that he was at least forty years of age and on the sixth step of their complex social ladder, then he could elect and be elected. To be elected, one had to have earned a position of leadership. To make a man responsible for the entire past history of the people also added weight to his thinking process. All in all, she supposed the system worked well for them.

Satisfied that she had done her best and that the collective best would be done for her, she stood up and looked to the south. Several Grant's gazelle stood there, silently, watching her without fear. "They know I am nothing but a quiet and gentle woman," she thought, admiring their delicate markings. Two white stripes ran down either side of their noses; the long eyelashes shielded liquid dark eyes from the rays of the hot sun and from too much dust. The horns of the male swept majestically upwards and outwards. His flanks were of a pale tawny brown, his belly a startling white. How proud he stood there, with the three females browsing nearby.

They were smaller and daintier, flaunting on each side an almost-black stripe. Their horns were shorter, though gracefully curved. "One man with three wives," Hawecha mused. "I wonder what that would be like."

The male stood there still and tall and then abruptly turned his back on her. He had sensed her presence. His rump was shining white, immaculate. The tail was white, with a black tip. He bounded off and away from her with a high kick of his hoofs. The females followed suit. They disappeared into the bushes, well camouflaged from further viewing.

"Time to return, I suppose," Hawecha thought. She rose, patted the grave in farewell and turned towards the settlement.

# CHAPTER 19

The women were waiting for her and descended upon her much as the plague of locusts had once landed upon ancient Egypt and devoured everything in sight.

"What was it like, standing there before our leaders?"

"Were you not ashamed at your own presumption?"

"Had you no care for the rest of us here?"

"What will become of womanhood now?"

Hawecha was taken aback. Had they no dignity then? Were they so submissive that everything a man said or did was right? She had hoped for some support, a *'Poor Hawecha!'* or even *'I will look after you now.'* Instead she was being rebuked and chastised by them all.

"I await the decision of the leaders of our illustrious people. I have given the matter to them. Will you not allow me peace and quiet until they have determined what to do with me?"

Her quiet voice impressed them. One by one, they left her.

"One day, I will teach the women," Hawecha decided. "Not how to disobey the men, of course. That was done by old Queen Haba Noyeh. And look what happened to her. In the end, the men lured her into a covered pit. When she fell in, they speared her to death. No, I will not teach disobedience." She walked around the settlement, seeing nothing.

"I will teach the women to make neater leatherwork and to sew cowries onto leather with minute stitches. That is easy, and women can gossip whilst they are learning. I have good fingers. They will respect that." Once more, she circumnavigated the perimeter.

"Next, I will teach them to wash babies properly. I have noticed they don't all wash their babies' bottoms well. When there is plenty of water, they must keep the babies clean." She reversed and walked in the opposite direction.

"Making herself tired," her female observers decided. "Let her walk her head off. She will need a long rest when the men are done with her."

Now her thoughts turned to husbands and wives and how they should treat each other. "With respect and decency, not with forcefulness or shouting." By the time she had walked around the compound seven times, she had exhausted her supply of ideas.

That evening, Gatto asked her to help prepare the evening meal. Three visitors had arrived and Gatto herself was tired. The evening passed with an entirely submissive Hawecha performing any task she was given. The old man watched her. At last, she was allowed to go to bed. She had achieved her goal. Worry and work had worn her out.

The next two days were days of sheer frustration. The elders still sat beneath their tree and returned to their homes long after dusk. They were tied by vows of silence. There was no gossip with which to titillate sharp tongues.

The women were shy with Hawecha, not quite knowing where to place her within their hierarchy. She nodded to them all, old or very young. Speech was beyond her. It was the loneliest period of her life. "Never again," she vowed. "When this is over, no matter the outcome, I will make myself very popular."

In the late afternoon of the third day, her uncle came to fetch her. He seemed older and quieter.

"The crows were right," the Father of the Assembly announced as she once more appeared before him. "They spoke of arguments and dissent and we have argued until we have no arguments left." He also seemed worn out.

"Stand still while I tell you what has been decided. I am too tired to deal with a fidget."

Indeed, in her nervousness, Hawecha had been grinding the sand beneath her right foot and twisting her goatskin skirts about her fingers. At his remonstrance, she clasped her hands behind her back, put her two feet together and waited for him to speak further. Now, she would hear her destiny.

"We have decided that you are not to blame for the failure of your marriage. All that we hear of your behaviour defines you as a good and obedient wife. We cannot find either Juldess or Godanna, so we cannot punish them. Let them find a new life together and make the best of it." Hawecha relaxed her neck and shoulders, grown tense with anxiety.

"As for you, dear child," he smiled at her for the first time, in a truly paternal manner. "As for you, we have all agreed that the marriage is annulled. You are free to return to the home of your birth, where you have relatives still who will care for you. Jarso-The-Councillor accepts you as one of his daughters, returned to him. He and Galgalu will cherish you until you are ready to make your own way in life."

Hawecha's heart warmed at this good news. Despite all his mannerisms, Jarso was now showing his true worth. The old man cleared his throat. He paused for a while before continuing, as if weighing his words most carefully.

"It is said that you had a vision when you were very young and that, had the villagers listened, you might have saved quite a few lives. Visions are beyond my province: the high priests are experts in this matter. One of them, a truly Holy Spirit amongst us, sees an aura about your forehead." Hawecha had heard of auras, but had not imagined she had one — or at least not one worth noticing.

"Before this multitude of men-folk, he swore that he saw a band of red and blue and green, passing around and around your head. He recognizes you as a Dreamer." Hawecha felt a tightening in her throat. The old man invited the high priest to speak.

A tall and immensely dignified old man rose from the front ranks of the elders. It was the first time Hawecha had seen one of their high priests. He was conscious of his role, yet there was no false pride in him. His face was gentle and serene as a child's. Hawecha noticed that he had exceedingly large and gnarled hands. The fingers encircled his stick much as an old vine entwines itself about a tree. The man and his staff of office seemed to belong together.

Taking centre stage now, the high priest spoke. His voice was clear as a bell, designed to carry to the very edges of a great crowd. He bowed towards an elder in the first rank — a man who stood out in the crowd by the very nature of his apparel.

Amongst all the men who were clothed in goatskins, he wore sparkling white. A long straight robe covered his body to his ankles. It had long sleeves, reaching down to his wrists. On his feet were strong leather sandals — heavier than the ones worn by Oromo people. The most remarkable thing about him though was the large white turban wrapped carefully about his head. His nose was proud, his beard neatly trimmed, almost as white as his headgear. His forehead was deeply seamed with years and years of living. Who could this man be?

"I greet the honourable Imam, the Muslim high priest who has come from the north, and who graces us with his wisdom. He has helped me reach my decision. Like me, he is considered a Holy Man whose word is law. I thank him for his help." He bowed towards their guest once more.

"In the matter of Hawecha, I depended first upon my own inner vision, for which I am well-known," the high priest continued. "I have had much experience with visions myself and recognize a true one from a false one."

Hawecha longed to escape from the position of prominence she had been forced to take, standing there once more before the leaders. She might as well be naked, the way they studied her. Was her nose too large, or her hair unkempt? Did they find her boastful, or arrogant in her pose? For a long time she had to be the centre of their attention. There was nothing for it. She had to remain there, standing stiff as a ramrod.

"When a high priest or other holy person is born, there are often omens which must be read by those experienced in such matters. Sometimes, colours fill up the sky over the new-born babe, as a signal to others that a special birth has occurred." He paused for breath.

"I am advised that Hawecha's birth was entirely ordinary and normal. Yet I see that she has a role to play, although I do not know what that role shall be. Only time and the passage of years will help her find spiritual self. The Imam and I both find her well motivated and truthful."

Now the high priest turned and spoke directly to Hawecha, piercing deep into her soul.

"The way is hard at times, Hawecha. Do not glory in this. God will send you many, many tests, to make sure you are good enough for Him.

You must lead a pure and simple life and obey the Creator in every way. Not many are chosen. Those who are, are never free from care and worry. The responsibilities are so great. The lives of many depend on them." His words fell into her heart, stone upon stone, promising her a difficult and even turbulent future. She could not look away. Her eyes were as if glued to his.

"In conclusion, Hawecha," the sage continued, "I urge you to be grateful to your aunt and uncle. At your age, women are no longer the responsibility of the elderly." He turned and walked slowly back to his seat. Hawecha noticed that one of his feet was badly splayed: one toe widely separated from the others. He limped a little. Poor man, to be so kind and have such pain She longed to make it better.

The Father of the Assembly arose, adjusted his goatskins, and once more addressed them all.

"Hawecha, we have studied the matter of your marriage from every point of view. We have argued over it mightily. Look about you, child. There are many great and wise men here."

He pointed them out to her. On his left sat two clan leaders. On his right sat a representative of the Supreme Traditional Governing Council, two councillors and a keeper of the wells. Lastly, his stick rested in the direction of a younger man, of humble expression and kind eyes. "My own firstborn son is sitting here. He is present to learn our ways. He must know how to conduct himself at such meetings. One day, when I have joined our ancestors, my son will succeed me. He will sit upon the sacred stool during his term of office. My fellow high priests have already approved of him."

Hawecha was overawed. She had no idea that so many great ones had joined in the deliberations over her life. "Suleh, help me, lest I faint!" A shaft of sunlight struck her upón the forehead. And with it came new strength.

The Father of the Assembly sat down. "My last words, I deliver from this sacred stool, so that Hawecha may take them seriously." He shook his stick at her and regarded her sternly. "One more thing, Hawecha and upon this one thing all the mighty souls here with us are entirely and absolutely agreed. You must never, never, never marry again! Do you understand, girl?" He shook his stick at her — the stick of his ancestors and Hawecha felt them all admonishing her. She gulped and nodded, too stunned to speak.

"Go now from us, Hawecha and live quietly with your aunt and uncle until God calls you. Until then, make sure you live a life of peace. Trouble us no more."

# CHAPTER 20

It was a fine and sparkling morning, the fifth since the Assembly had ended with a prayer for peace for the world. One by one, families had dispersed, carrying news of all the happenings to the four corners of Liban.

Old Jarso was more morose than ever, sunk into a depression that seemed beyond healing. Iridescent spider-webs spangled with morning dew-drops, a tiny white flower-bud opening up beside them on the path, a tremor of leaves, an orange dawn: none of this had aroused him or impressed him with its splendour. They were surrounded by magnificence; yet from Jarso came not one word.

Hawecha could do nothing to draw him out from his despair. Nor could she see how she could have offended him. There was nothing to do but enjoy what was there to be enjoyed. She began to count the clouds. Some were wispy, whilst some were dense puffballs. Others swept across the sky with long fingers. There was much to occupy her mind.

Retracing their steps, they came to the village where Jarso had made himself so unpopular on the outward journey. He bowed to his host, Dabo, and sank down upon the log that separated the bedroom from the eating area. An appalling breach of etiquette. Was he ill, then? They gave him water, stretched him out upon the bed and fanned him with a woven grass platter. He fell into a gentle sleep. "His emotions have worn him out," old Dabo commented, excusing his behaviour.

Jarso seemed to have recovered by the following morning. Once more, they loaded up their donkeys and set off homewards. He sat a little straighter. Other than that, there was no change. He turned his head neither to left nor to right. He did not enquire as to Hawecha's well-being, nor her feelings, nor her ability to keep up. He led the way; she followed. For two more days. She felt herself grow smaller.

The sun sat high in the heavens. The landscape flattened out in its merciless glare, all colour bleached out of it. The air shimmered and danced. Their leather bag for water was almost empty.

At last, as if floating in the ether, their own village could be perceived ahead. The mirage made it seem closer than it was. Another hour or so elapsed before they came to the entrance. Hawecha had not known what sort of welcome to expect. But surely not this silence? She shuffled wearily into the hut.

Galgalu lay spread-eagled upon her bed in heat-prostrated stupor. Hawecha nudged her gently into wakefulness. Galgalu struggled into an upright position, patted her hair into a semblance of order, yawned widely, straightened her leather skirts, stood and bowed before her husband. Then, having attended to her wifely duties, she took Hawecha by the hands. "I am so very glad to have you back, my dear. It has been very lonely without you."

Gazing into her aunt's eyes, Hawecha saw nothing but love there, and genuine concern. "The girl is so thin, now. What have you done to her?"

"Hawecha is nothing but trouble," Jarso grumbled, making his feelings plain for the first time. "The Father forbids her to marry again. We are saddled with her for the rest of our lives." He turned towards the doorway. "And what is more, I shall have to return the bride-price. I am no longer rich." He stalked out of the hut to inform the men-folk. From them, he would get some sympathy.

Hawecha shrugged her shoulders helplessly. "Give him time, my dear," Galgalu advised. "He often gets this way. His pride is badly pricked. He has to have his say. Just keep quiet and busy. You'll see. He'll come round eventually."

One by one, the women came to enquire as to Hawecha's welfare. The younger ones were openly curious. Everyone was interested in the lawmakers' settlement. How many huts? How many people? How far away was it and in which direction? Had she made any friends there? Had she really met an Imam?

Poor Hawecha had been largely involved in her own personal destiny and could not always answer well enough. Yet their attention pleased her and she made every effort to respond. After all, their daily lives were routinely rather dull. She had become a major source of information.

The ice broke. Jarso's silence broke. The village returned to normal.

# CHAPTER 21

Hawecha sat in the hut, with her mother's ceremonial objects strewn about her. She would never wear the round brass shoulder-ornament worn by the mother of a *gadamoji*. She would never have a son, alas! What was to be done with it? She would have to put it away until a suitable recipient came forward. Someone else would bear a son.

Suddenly, she thought of Dabassah. She had seen little of him in the past three weeks, so preoccupied had she been with her own affairs. Hawecha felt ashamed.

"Father, are you within?" she called, tapping gently with a stick upon the framework of his doorway. A feeble voice bid her enter.

Absence had sharpened her eyes. As they grew accustomed to the inner darkness, Hawecha realised for the first time just how old he was now. Far, far older than her uncle: in fact, older than anyone she had met. His eyes glowed in a face that was almost cadaverous. Every rib stuck out of his narrow, bony chest. His hands resembled the claws of a crow. His hump seemed even larger.

His hut, though swept, was untidy. It was clearly beyond him to take care of himself. Hawecha set about straightening his few possessions. It was not right that he, who gave the village so much, should live alone now. Thoughts chased each other furiously around her head.

She marched back to her own home and without preamble attacked her aunt and uncle on this issue. "My uncle, you have my aunt to take care of you. Everybody in this village has a somebody. Only our teacher is alone. It is not fair or right!" she wailed. "I want to live with him. Please allow this."

Much to her amazement, Jarso sighed, nodded his head and capitulated at once. No battle, no tears, no pleading. She packed up her few belongings, promised to visit at least once a day, and hastily re-established herself on the opposite side of the compound.

For three years, she tended to Dabassah's needs. He in return treated her as his daughter. A great fondness developed between them. Gradually, Dabassah began to teach her, bequeathing to her the sum total of his herbal knowledge. He spoke of those that grew nearby and of many that grew in other places: ones that Hawecha would most likely never see. She tried to remember all their names — to please him. In her heart, she knew she would fail. He took her with him on his early morning rambles — much shorter now — not to find new plants (for he had by now exhausted those available) but to introduce her to the matter of omens.

"Look up at the sky and study that small cloud. It speaks, Hawecha. It speaks!" Obediently she would stare at it, until the message came through. "Look after him well in his last days. Love him for his knowledge." She quivered, and silently promised.

Under his direction, she would contemplate a star, or study a winding snake-track across the path. Three dark leaves meant thus and so. This bent stick would reveal its hidden message if she studied it. She became better and better at it.

Until one day, she simply found her attention drawn to a particular cloud overhead, or to a specific sign. She realised she had grown up now and no longer needed his coaching. She begged him to teach her the sandals. So many people needed help in interpreting their future.

Desultorily, Dabassah complied, taking off his ancient, shabby pair and casting them dejectedly upon the ground. "I have no strength left, girl," he moaned. "You will have to try very hard to follow this."

Hawecha understood that the future depended upon the way in which the sandals fell. Did they both point in the same direction? Did they lie side by side? Was one atop the other and if so, which one lay uppermost? She tried, but Dabassah had reached a point where he rarely completed a sentence. His mind began to wander. She knew that he would die soon.

The day came. She found him asleep in his bed, one sandal clutched in his right hand. Hawecha flung herself upon her knees and sobbed. She had lost her second father. When the tears would flow no more, she walked steadily towards the hut of Harero-The-Spiritual-Leader — to announce the great loss. Harero took the news to Buleh.

Buleh took it badly. "No Great Laugh today, that is for sure." He swayed and rocked in silent grief, remembering the long ago joke. No doubt his own death loomed closer now.

When his thoughts had run their course, Harero looked at Hawecha. "You will have to do it then. You will have to teach whatever you can now. You must know something, girl. Well, do you?"

Much taken aback both at his question and at the unprecedented sharpness of his words, Hawecha explained her utter failure to master the art of throwing sandals and her complete confidence in the matter of making herbal remedies.

"I appoint you then as his successor," Harero announced. "From father to son, the knowledge passes usually." He nodded his head vigorously. "Yes, and sometimes from mother to .... to daughter." Hawecha waited patiently.

"His goats belong to you now," Harero continued. "Yes, yes. His goats. And his hut also. Yes, he would have liked that."

Hawecha had expected no reward, whatsoever, and certainly not such riches.

"He always said one day you would prove yourself. Take whatever he has." Harero turned his head skywards as if searching the heavens for further input. The minutes passed.

Hawecha hemmed and cleared her throat.

"Oh what? Ah .... yes. It is you. Chosen. Yes, yes. Enough. I have spoken."

# CHAPTER 22

"Make it better, Hawecha. Make it even better."

Hawecha turned in her sleep and attempted to sweep the dream aside. The voice persisted. "Hawecha, make his work even better!"

She thrust away deep sleep and slid rapidly into consciousness. The voice had been that of Sirius. What other advice had there been? A faint glimmering of shooting stars, a finger pointing north, a shimmering leaf of a plant unknown to her; a medicinal one, it seemed.

Outside, it was still dark. Sirius shone brightly overhead, near to Orion, and at the edge of the Milky Way. "Tell me more. I need to know more," Hawecha thought. Yet nothing more came forwards.

Hawecha paced about the compound, wondering precisely what her dream had meant. At last, it came to her that if she travelled northwards, she would find a new medicinal plant. The dream had been so simple. Then confusion fell once more. How far north? Should she load up her donkey? Would somebody else have to look after her newly acquired goats?

It was three days since they had buried Dabassah. She had barely become adjusted to being a woman of property. Nor had she begun any work. At a time like this, nobody would have expected her to practise her healing arts. She would announce when she was ready.

Well, it seemed Sirius was telling her that she was ready, or that at least she must make headway. She decided that if a donkey had been needed, she would have dreamed of it. That was how her dreamworld functioned.

At daybreak, she took up Dabassah's stick and a small leather pouch, as well as a small water-bag. As the sun rose, she turned at right angles to it and boldly set out on her quest.

By noon, she had not recognised the plant of her dream. She had seen the large white shell of a land-snail, which had simply advised her to continue. She had noticed the footprints of goats in the sand: they had told her to stand still and listen. Doing so, she had heard a pigeon cooing: "Stand still, stand still some more." A kite had flown down from a large tree and encircled her head. "Walk straight on," it had shrilled.

Hawecha paused in the shade of a large bush, to take a few sips of water and rest awhile. Quests were hard. It seemed no omen ever advised one to rest. Just then, a blue and orange lizard slithered up to the top of a rock and eyed her calmly. "You may rest for a while. The journey is not long now, however. You might prefer to end it."

Her curiosity aroused, Hawecha looked to left and right and then stood up again. She turned to the right and spotted not far off, a small heap of boulders, tossed carelessly upon the landscape by some ancient earthly upheaval. Perhaps from a small hill that stood blue-clad upon the horizon. Something about the rocks drew her attention sharply. She approached them.

There, behind the heap of rocks was a small shrub, with silvery-green leaves, which — as in her dream — shimmered in the strong sunlight. Hawecha knelt down to understand it better. She plucked off one of its leaves and held it to her nostrils. No aroma. A soft and silky feeling. Gradually, the information came. A herbal remedy for women, to use when suffering from cramps. Stronger than the one she knew of. This was the strongest in the area.

Hawecha listened carefully, her mind recording useful facts. Three leaves brewed up for half an hour. Cool ... and drink.

"How often?" she asked. "Only once a day. Evening is best. Once a day is enough."

How was she to take the plant home with her? She walked around to see if others of this species grew nearby, and was greatly relieved to find three more. Carefully, as Dabassah had taught her, she dug up the first plant, roots and all. She wrapped it carefully in her pouch, with a little of the surrounding soil. Then she turned to the east and asked the sun to bless the plant and to help it grow outside her hut. She hoped it would. If not, she would have to return here and cull the leaves when necessary.

Later, much later, when the plant had been carefully planted to the right of her doorway and watered heavily, Hawecha remembered the lizard and thanked him; and Sirius, and all her other omens. All who had helped her on her quest.

Weeks later, a young woman passed by to complain of the heat and how difficult it was to carry a baby around when your belly ached so badly. Hawecha took this as a sign that she was to prepare her new medicine forthwith. Two days later, the young woman came to thank her.

Bonsa-The-Gentle was her second patient. Several others followed. Within a short while, Hawecha found herself quite busy.

One day, she realised she was happy. She walked around with her head held high and a smile upon her lips. Snatches of old songs danced around in her head. Hawecha had found herself. They all noticed, of course; Hawecha-The-Healer had begun.

# CHAPTER 23

The word soon spread, and Hawecha found herself treating everything from thorns deeply embedded in a thick-soled foot to a headache that lasted several days. Coughs, colds and chest pains were frequent complaints. The most common by far were "women's problems". Hawecha's periods had simply ceased after her visit to the Assembly. She took this as a gift from God to make her work much easier. There was more strength in her than in the average female. She used that extra strength to the full, working from dawn well into the night.

Women liked coming to her. She sat them down in the cool of her hut and listened patiently to their stories. She shut her eyes, tried to see the ailment and imagined putting her fingers on the site of the inflammation, or on the internal organ that was the source of pain. Healing came naturally to her. The more she studied it, the more she learned.

Every night, when the day's work was ended, she would sit quietly outside the hut, with her eyes tightly shut. "Great God, if you have something more to teach me, now is the time." Every night, she received a different set of instructions.

"That healing plant will be much stronger for you if you breathe onto it three times before you pluck the leaves." The plant outside her doorway did indeed seem to increase in potency, providing swifter relief for the many women who needed its soothing properties.

"Lift up your head, and talk to the stars. They are all ready to help you now!" and, obediently, Hawecha would raise her eyes to the vast sweep of heaven above and seek out the bright twinkle that held a message for her. There were uncountable, innumerable stars there: enough for innumerable messages!

By now, Hawecha lived in a Half-World, assisted by God, the stars, birds and omens, as well as the knowledge Dabassah had bequeathed her. In addition, insights and solutions frequently came to her in her dreams.

Over a particularly troublesome case, Hawecha sometimes thrashed around in her sleep, as if looking for the cure. Upon awakening, she would remember her tormented night and with it find the answer.

Women came from nearby villages, as much as a day's journey away. Old and young, married or not and mothers carrying their ailing children. Hawecha dealt with them all, growing in joy and serenity.

One night, the message from God pertained to men — or rather to one man in particular. "Look at the way he turns his head, Hawecha. You will see the stiffness inside his neck. See where to put your healing hands, if he decides to ask for help." That advice was for old Jarso.

How could she help her uncle? Her patients were all women. It was many months before he asked if she could take his pain away. She knew exactly where to place her hands to relieve the tension. As an added precaution, she gave him a decoction made up of two plants. One was a muscle relaxant: the other was meant to soften pride.

Three doses and Jarso proclaimed himself much better. It was true. He could bend his head forward and backward and from side to side without grimacing. Hawecha knew he was completely cured. She could feel her heart swell. Maybe now the men would also come.

She soon discovered that most were reluctant to receive help from her. Only a few of the elderly called on her for healing. Perhaps by now their hearts had softened with much living and they were more accepting of her talents. Or had they less pride than the younger age-set that held all the political power? Hawecha could only wait.

Some clients were far beyond Hawecha's powers to help. One might be too weakened by amoebic dysentery and too dehydrated to survive. In another, the cancer was too advanced for any cure within Hawecha's pharmacopoeia or insights. Frequently, the patient was just too old.

In these hopeless cases, Hawecha would half-shut her eyes, and see the truth: a broken silver cord, with the soul already flying about somewhere above in the ethers, waiting for release and freedom. Hawecha lived more and more often with Death, which she saw as a great black shadow overhead. She knew that spirit friends were hovering about, waiting to assist the soul into the after-life.

She had seen this world in one of her "Great Dreams" as she called them. A land of gentle hills and gentle light, bathed in an other-worldly softness. The grass was of an unearthly green, brighter beyond the brightest newborn leaflet. There, the trees were large, many-branched and thick with leaves, casting enough shadow for an entire village to live beneath. Rainbows shimmered in the distance, even though no rain had fallen. The sun shone brightly but gently; it had different powers from those it had on earth.

The small clouds that had scudded across her vision were all tinged with pink, and rose ... and gold. Hawecha was particularly enthralled by colours. From the wild flowers, she knew red and orange, pink and violet, white and yellow. Birds gave her brighter flashes or deeper variations of these hues. The sky above was of many different shades of blue. Earth and vegetation provided her with variations of brown and green. Water could sparkle like silver and the stars reminded her of that. Metal bangles shone like silver. Silver, she knew very well. Her Colour-World was rich.

But in all that world, it was only the sun that resembled gold. She studied the sun now, closing her eyes to protect them from the violence of its rays, and tuning in at an inner level. There was no message there, however. Only warmth and beauty. She wondered why her dream clouds had been edged with this gold. Again, there were no answers.

Months passed, and then one day Hawecha became aware of the fact that every human being had colours dancing around them, if you looked hard. She began to study this aura.

When somebody was in a bad mood, Hawecha saw the body surrounded by angry black and dirty yellow-brown. If a person had a stiff knee, there was a cloud of black around it. If a patient came who was close to death, the aura was hardly there. Just a narrow band of cold grey running close to the skin.

On the other hand, watching a mother bathing her baby in the river was a beauteous sight: a human rainbow of pink, mauve and translucent yellow. Her aunt was mostly bright yellow when studied in a half-light. Children were often a flash of cheeky red as they frolicked happily about, playing with stone donkeys and goats, or chasing each other around the compound. Their laughter sent out sparks of silver, red or brilliant blue.

Sometimes, Hawecha saw eyes that seemed to weep pure malice or send out waves of mischief. Once, a hand told her that its owner was lying. To her utter disbelief, a stomach spilled out deep and abiding yellow-green jealousy.

Hawecha had learned to not only see the colours of the aura, but also to interpret them accurately. She had learned to study character and to read the person's hidden truths — however unpleasant.

Her favourite colour was silver. Apart from the silver cord connecting spirit and matter, Hawecha often saw a quick flash of it in the aura, usually around the head and shoulders. It came and went swiftly, however. She understood it did not represent any of the normal human traits.

Her first glimpse of a complete silver aura was when a shy little girl with a club foot had sidled up to her and with atypical courage looked her straight in the eye and announced that when she grew up, she wanted to be just like her. At that moment, the girl had been completely hidden by bright silver, which sent out great long rays into the sky. The little girl had turned into the largest of all the stars.

Greatly moved, Hawecha knelt and hugged the child tightly to her, promising to teach her one day, when she had finished with all the normal lessons of a woman's daily life.

As she turned away, the meaning of silver suddenly overwhelmed her. It came when mind and spirit were one: when a person meant something with all their heart and soul. As if, at that precise moment, a seemingly insignificant human being had become much larger: a creature of astounding beauty. It was the purest and most spiritual self-expression there was. The soul 'spoke' as though it were truly a small piece of God. It was the colour of *spirituality*.

Alas, Hawecha's search for silver was seldom satisfied. It seemed that usually it was the mind and the body that ruled.

Gold was an even rarer sight. The first time she saw it in the aura, a young mother sat grieving beside the body of her baby — a boy born far too soon. Hawecha had assisted at the birth. It had been precipitous and the umbilical cord had been firmly caught around the baby's neck.

"Stop pushing!" Hawecha had instructed, as she attempted to extricate the child. Too late. As the child finally slipped into this world, Hawecha saw it's soul had already gone, carried upwards by Suleh and her three assistants.

It was the young woman's first-born. Hawecha had anticipated howls and shrieks of anguish. Instead, the woman sat with dignity beside the tiny body, with tears coursing silently down her polished cheeks. She rocked back and forth, her hands held calmly in her lap, whispering words of prayer.

> *"God, I give you my child. Please keep him happy!*
> *I give you this child to look after for me.*
> *May he grow big and strong. May he be really big!*
> *Find him friends to play with, please.*
> *Look after him for me, God!"*

It was then that Hawecha beheld the sheet of soft gold that covered the woman's face, the fronds and curlicues that emanated from her forehead and the golden sphere in which she sat. Hawecha understood that gold was the colour of *wisdom.*

One day when Hawecha sat on a stool milking her goat — about a year after she first began observing and analysing auras — she decided to turn her vision inwards and see if she could study her own auric field. She abandoned the milking, closed her eyes and concentrated on herself.

Bright violet feathers curled above her right eye. Pale blue — like the early evening sky — surrounded her. A red streak ran around her in a circle, at the level of her chest. Pale silvery-green spots flickered around her shoulders. She extended her vision outwards from her body, seeing splashes of yellow and spots of deep violet. A sheet of silver seemed to enfold her.

There it was! Much further out than she had imagined possible — the distance from her hut to the next. She sat in a sphere of gold. It was brighter than the gold of the bereaved young mother — more like the harsh sun at high noon than the evening sun that had lost much of its power. Hawecha sensed that a softer gold was preferable to a dazzling, blinding one, so she sat quietly and asked God to help her understand the difference.

"You are a little overbearing with your knowledge, skill and power. She is a far gentler soul. Try to be more like her."

Thus reprimanded, Hawecha resumed her milking determined to do better.

# CHAPTER 24

Jarso was found dead in his bed one morning. He had of late become quite muddle-headed and prone to nodding off quite suddenly. Nonetheless, his death came as a shock to the small community.

Galgalu aged visibly, turning overnight into a frail and aged crone. Hawecha knew her aunt desired only to follow her companion of many years and was prepared for a second sudden death. She moved back in with Galgalu and cut down on her healing practise, in order to take care of her.

Yet the second death came where she least expected it. Little Bonsa, the 'silver aura' whose one ambition had been to be Hawecha's disciple, developed an infection in her foot after stumbling onto a hot coal. Hawecha held the small misshapen foot in her hands and rubbed it with a soothing ointment made from crushed leaves mixed with a little cow fat. Over and over, she rubbed in the unguent, determined to stop the infection. Despite her efforts, the infection spread up Bonsa's leg and into her groin. She developed a fever, which did not respond to Hawecha's ministrations. Soaked in sweat, she lay on her bed tossing and turning. Then, quite suddenly, she sat up, gasped and fell back lifeless.

Three weeks later, Galgalu collapsed over her hearth stones. When Hawecha rushed to help, she saw the spark of life had gone. Hawecha sat there, too stunned to weep. Old Death had come too close and too often.

For a whole week, Hawecha mourned, forgetting to eat or drink; forgetting her patients. Overwhelmed by the transitory nature of life, Hawecha could do nothing.

One day, she awoke with the strong thought that she must visit Wareh-The-Diviner who lived more than a days' journey away. She needed to know her own future.

She took a little dried goat meat and a large leather bag full of water (for herself and her donkey) and a large wooden bowl to pour it into, so he could drink his fill. Turning towards the north-east, she set off, following a well-worn path through the bushland.

Too weary to notice omens, too emotionally exhausted to enjoy the sight of birds, clouds or wildflowers, she plodded onwards until day turned into night. Tethering her donkey to a small tree, she curled up under a small thornbush and found oblivion swiftly.

By noon the next day, she had arrived in Wareh's village and was shown where the old soothsayer lived. She sat down upon a wooden stool, hung her head dejectedly and waited.

Wareh was wise as well as wizened. She knew deep depression when she saw it. She instructed Hawecha to purchase a small quantity of coffee-beans from the woman in the village who traded them. Poor Hawecha realised that she had brought nothing with her to barter! Greatly embarrassed, she fingered a cowrie shell she wore on a thong round her neck for good luck, wondering if it would suffice. Cowries were much prized amongst her people, particularly amongst the women. For the young, it represented fertility, whilst for older women, it was said to increase their powers.

Wareh shook her head. "I see you too are a holy woman. Keep your cowrie. I will help you out of love."

She took from beneath her goatskin bedroll a small and worn old pouch. From it, she took eight coffee beans, to which she added a small pinch of salt stored in a nearby gourd. She closed her eyes and held her hand out over the fire, blessing the objects held in her open palm. For a long while, she was silent.

"You have great gifts, Hawecha," she began. "Well and truly, God has blessed you so that you may help our people. As the years pass by, you will help many with your healing arts and also with your divinations."

Hawecha looked up in surprise, for as yet she made none, nor had she ever thought to make predictions. Wareh recognised her astonishment.

"It is not in you yet, you have many dreams. The dreams are your key to the future – not coffee beans or sandals. Your mind is your greatest tool. Use it, and trust it and you cannot fail." Hawecha nodded, knowing that somehow old Wareh was right.

"You will travel far. Indeed, your whole life is one of movement. You will be much needed. I also see that you will be much loved and respected. There is not a home where you will not be welcome. All Liban is yours." Hawecha felt considerably better and sat up proudly on her stool.

Wareh sighed and opened her eyes, looking straight into Hawecha's. "There is a little bad news too, my dear. At times, you will be afraid. And — like me — at times you will be lonely."

Wareh understood that her own life would not be long now. Whereas she represented the past, Hawecha was the future. Perhaps she had frightened Hawecha too greatly. She must make amends and give her client more assurance. "Yours is a good and useful life, with much love in it. You will be greatly respected, even by the men-folk. You will be one of our shining souls. And, near the end of your life, you will teach. Life cannot always be happy. We have to pay for it. Grasp life while you can, and help wherever you can. Old and worn I see you, as you see me today. I have lived. I have no regrets. Make sure you can say the same, when life is ready to leave you. Live quietly, and do your work. They call you "The Chosen One". I see that it is true. Ask God to guide you. You are *his* child now."

Hawecha nodded. "It is true, Mother, for I have no other kin. My half-sisters live too far away. My head is in the stars. It is true. Only God can help me."

They sat there, far into the night — spiritual mother and spiritual daughter — exchanging ideas and insights, finding comfort in each other. For a while, at least, the loneliness and fear diminished. She returned to her village refreshed.

# CHAPTER 25

An eight-year cycle of Oromo culture came to an end and it was again time for one of the great *gadamoji* ceremonies. So far, Hawecha had not been invited to attend one. By now, however, her fame had spread as a wise woman and furthermore a sensitive one.

In the north, the high priest of the Odito Clan had been preparing himself for this one with particular care, for, given his age, it was unlikely he would be present at the next one. As his prayers increased in fervour and as he underwent his third coffee purification ritual, an uneasy feeling came over him. At first he shrugged it off, but the feeling was persistent. Something could go very wrong!

He withdrew to a small tree outside the compound, hoping for illumination. "Women. The trouble will come from the women." He pondered further, asking for a way to prevent this trouble. The *gadamoji* ceremony was a sacred event. Disturbances could bring misfortune upon them all.

At last, he understood that without a strong figure in authority, the women would quarrel amongst themselves. He had heard of Hawecha, of course. Hawecha-The-Chosen-One was the only person who could be entrusted to keep the women in order. He knew the four other high priests would not object. He sent a messenger to locate her and bring her without undue delay.

Thus, for the second time in her life, Hawecha stood with a bowed head before one of the most respected leaders of her people. He told her he entrusted her with the responsibility of keeping peace among the women.

"I bless you and call upon you. Do not fail me, child."

It was a greatly subdued Hawecha who returned to her village for the three months remaining before the ceremony was due to begin.

As the time approached, Hawecha realised that she should undergo a purification and that to do so, a coffee ritual was mandatory. She invited the two oldest women in her village to join her. They sat companionably around her fire.

Old Taditi-The-Pure cracked a handful of coffee beans open with her teeth and threw them into a small clay pot, together with a little cow fat. She stirred the mixture slowly. Hawecha scooped it into her large wooden bowl full of goat milk which had reached a near-boil over the fire. The coffee beans sizzled. She poured the mixture into three small wooden cups. Kneeling before Taditi, Hawecha offered her one. Taditi prayed for peace to fall upon them all and then proceeded to sip.

Hawecha took the second cup to Terri-The-Best-Milker and knelt before her also as Terri prayed for peace at the ceremonies. The three women sat in silence, sipping away at the holy brew, until all the coffee was finished. She was left alone.

Hawecha sensed the ritual had done her much good. Her aura felt brighter and lighter. She straightened her back and felt supremely confident. From then onwards, she would always use coffee to restore her sense of balance.

She still felt confident when the time for departure came. Many assembled to bid her farewell, wished her well and gave many small gifts of salt, tobacco and grain.

On the second day of her journey, she was given a small pouchful of *tef*. This grain had come to Liban from further north and seeds had been planted in several of the local villages. Unfortunately, it had not flourished. Old Jarso had long ago decided it 'did not like Liban' and after three crops had failed, had happily returned to the finger millet of his ancestors. Hawecha was therefore surprised to find *tef* still available. She tucked it away with her other gifts and possessions.

The paths to Arero grew more and more crowded, as families made their way towards the traditional place of ceremony. As Hawecha neared her destination, the crowds pressed thicker about her. The whole world was on the move.Young boys helped drive the herds of goats forwards, whilst their older brothers dealt with the great-horned cattle. Donkeys turned to stare at her — a woman on her own — as if to tell her this was unseemly. She laughed at their reproachful faces.

"I am Hawecha, you know!"

Little girls ran up to clutch at her skirts as she passed by, her head held high, with a great sense of spiritual purpose to sustain her. Young women bowed their heads as she rode past them. Despite her relative youth, she was beyond the normal hierarchy. Hawecha rejoiced in the goodness of life: not for one moment was she lonely.

The ceremonial village was vast, with many, many huts already constructed. Unlike those of the lawmakers' settlement, these formed one great semi-circle, facing eastwards. Many of them were inter-connected from the inside, resembling long, low rabbit warrens. Large families could thus remain under one roof together with all their guests. There existed a hierarchical order, with two ritual leaders presiding. Their huts were to the far left.

The village was enclosed by the usual thick protective thornbush enclosure. In the eastern wall, ceremonial gates had been left open — each gap representing one of the old men who would shortly become a *gadamoji*.

Within the large enclosure, individual enclosures had been built to house the small livestock. Cattle were kept in a large communal area. To the rear, a separate enclosure housed a few camels. Hawecha headed straight for this enclosure.

How proud they stood and how high! What a long shadow they cast upon the earth! She watched as one nibbled on a bit of thorn, admiring the way its whole lower jaw seemed to slither sideways as it ate. She came a little closer to one, to admire its long eyelashes. Just then, the camel let out a great fart and gurgled alarmingly. Hawecha drew back hastily. So much for 'nobility' and 'greatness'!

She settled in with a kindly family, low down on the social ladder, and therefore situated far to the right. Having fetched water from the communal well, Hawecha asked for permission to explore further and after being relieved of her duties, she set off towards the eastern wall, with all its ceremonial exits.

On the inside of each gate, the wife of each elder who would become a *gadamoji* had constructed a mound of cow dung, with the top hollowed out to form a shallow bowl. On the outside of the gate another pile had been erected, this one high-domed. At the third heap an old woman was proudly patting the dung into a more perfect shape. Hawecha asked her what they were for.

The woman — eager to show off her superior knowledge — explained that each *gadamoji* would have his hair shaved off by his wife the next day. The hair would be buried in the inner dung-heap — called a *dobbu* — in front of his ceremonial gateway. The outer heap was called a *foddu*. Every morning, the wife would add dung to it and every morning her husband and their son would squat beside it and pray together.

Warming to her subject, the woman who introduced herself as Khaloh explained that the move to this place had begun with the sighting of the new moon a month before, in the month of *buufa*. Because of the wind that blew during that month, it was named after the blacksmith's bellows.

Now, a month later, the new moon had been sighted the night before. Being the month known as *wachabaji*, it was time to begin the celebrations.

Eyeing her now perfect dung-heap with satisfaction, Khaloh rocked back on her heels and continued. The celebration was a family affair and several other ceremonies would follow this one. Two first-born sons would be named in separate ceremonies. Later — outside the compound in a smaller settlement — another special ceremony would take place for all the first-born children. Khaloh advised Hawecha to stay for three months, if she wished to do her job well.

Hawecha was greatly perturbed. Keeping peace among the women for a few days was a task she could well handle but three months was another matter. Coffee, coffee, coffee. That would be her solution. "I'd better begin my job at once!" she cried and headed for the open savannah beyond the compound. She needed time to think.

Idly plucking at tall grasses and twirling them about in her fingers, Hawecha found her answer. It lay not in repeated coffee rituals but rather in calling the women to prayer. If they were united in this, perhaps they would remain united through all the pressures that would be placed upon them. Petty squabbles would surely be avoided; jealousy would be prevented; competing for attention would be minimized. Yes, repeated prayers were most assuredly the answer.

Returning to the village in the late afternoon, Hawecha apologised to her hostess for not having been of much use to her. "You do your work, and I'll do mine," was Djataneh's sensible comment. Thus, with a fair division of labour apportioned between them, Hawecha settled down for the night.

# CHAPTER 26

After the morning gruel, Hawecha set to work. She had decided to organise a prayer meeting for that very night, after the evening meal. The women would be busy putting the finishing touches to their ceremonial finery and preparing themselves for their participation in the ceremony. There would be no time for the coffee ritual she had come to love.

First she paid her respects to the two ritual leaders, offering to help in any way she could. She explained that she needed a suitable place for her evening prayer. Where did the Fathers suggest?

The elder of the two, a man with piercing eyes and haughty demeanour, pointed eastwards to a large shady thorn tree growing beyond the village and explained that it was the elder's tree, specifically designated for their meetings and advised her to keep well away from it. Nor could she go anywhere near the tree the clan elders had recently proclaimed sacred. It had been anointed with coffee, tobacco, myrrh and milk. They had tied onto its branches small strips of hide taken from a goat that had been sacrificed for this purpose. Every morning, the elders would gather there and pray for peace. That tree was taboo. No woman could approach it. Having completed his sermon, he turned from her and walked away.

The other man, milder and gentler by nature, took up where the first had left off. He pointed to the west of the compound and suggested she select a tree 'out there' far away from trouble.

Hawecha wandered about until she found an ideal spot. Not one large tree, but three smaller ones. The trees created a sheltering environment. The place had an aura of holiness about it. Well pleased with her choice, she set off to inform the women.

She came up to a group of three who were busily mending and sewing. One was working on the leather ornament which would be tied to her wrist; from it dangled the tops of seven or eight small gourds: these would clatter against each other as she walked. Another woman was re-attaching dangles to the leather apron she would wear hanging down her back. The third was stitching cowries onto a leather bandolier her husband would wear across his chest during their son's naming ceremony.

In another part of the village, two young mothers were washing their babies. Others were sweeping the area outside their huts. There was a tremendous 'to-ing' and 'fro-ing,' as women borrowed extra salt from a neighbour, asked for help from a friend, hired each other's daughters for the most menial tasks, or fetched and carried more water.

Wherever she went, Hawecha was given warm greetings. It seemed the decisions made by the high priest at the lawmakers' gathering held far-reaching consequences for her. She was called 'Suleh's daughter' by one aged grandmother. Another old woman hailed her as 'the one born of no parents'.

Although these stories were fictitious, she decided she might as well enjoy them. After all, her parents had died when she was very small indeed. Her foster parents had by now also died. She had no living grandparents. Her one child had died at birth. Her husband had left her and she had been forbidden to marry again. There were no generations behind or before her. So who were her family?

She felt she belonged 'up there' with the First Five Teachers of the Oromo people, Suleh, and all the Oromo heroes, and that her earthly ties were unimportant. She had changed so greatly in the last four years. Perhaps in a way she no longer belonged with people. The Chosen Ones of Oromo history always lived alone with their thoughts and prayers. So, in a sense, the stories were right.

None of the women refused her call to prayer, although several could not promise they would attend, because of other duties. Hawecha made her rounds, cajoling and pleading her cause. At a certain stage, she knew she could do no more.

By now it was mid-morning. A special ceremony was due to begin. Hawecha had asked if she might witness it and permission had been granted.

According to custom, if an elder had died before reaching the exalted state of *gadamoji*, his widow performed a substitute ceremony in his place. Before she could do so, it was customary to depict her dead husband's heroic exploits by painting these onto a large cowhide which was mounted on the outside wall of the widow's hut.

Hawecha watched as the elder's three sons set to work with white chalk purchased from traders of the neighbouring Konso tribe. It seemed the father had been a great hero in local lore. His sons sought to do him great honour.

Slowly, with great care and attention to detail, a large elephant was drawn with enormous tusks and baleful eye. The deceased had in his youth speared this fearsome beast to death and all by himself, it transpired. Next, a leopard appeared. Beside it, a crudely-drawn man lay dead upon the ground: a Konso, it was said. Now that these exploits had been depicted for all the world to admire, the widow could proceed with the rituals.

Earlier that morning, the family had slaughtered a cow in the centre of the cattle enclosure. The meat had already been cut up and distributed. The cowhide had been drawn over the head, feet and entrails.

A branch had been pulled out from the ceremonial gateway and this was used to weigh down the remains, to prevent vultures from swooping down to eat. It also kept at bay the villager's dogs – small, barrel-chested and sandy-beige in colour with scattered white splotches.

Six of the *gadamoji* now appeared inside the enclosure. They made their way towards the ceremonial gateway of their deceased age mate, passed through it, turned around and then headed in single file to the widow's hut.

Outside it, the eldest son recited in poetic words the saga of his father's heroism. The men shouted "seize it!" and disappeared into the hut. They emerged suddenly carrying a large milk container woven from the roots of the wild asparagus plant and decorated with cowries. The widow led the procession to the remains of the cow and the men squatted beside it. The widow scooped out a little soured milk from the milk container; each elder sipped from this in turn.

Alone, the widow walked to her *dobbu* and buried a handful of tobacco in the hollowed-out basin-shaped top. She then shaped it into a dome. The woman wept as she did this.

Returning from this moving ritual, Hawecha saw that all the *gadamoji* families were now engaged in drawing and painting. One by one, the cowhides were affixed to the huts for all to see. Hawecha walked along the great arc of dwellings to enjoy the depicted prowess: another elephant, a rhino, two more leopards and several giraffes. Their entrails lay exposed, their blood spilled on the ground. The degree of artistry and skill was admirable. These gory scenes leapt to life before her.

Admiring the rhino, she saw a man of exceptional age lost in thought before it. He leaned heavily on a rough stick and nodded his head repeatedly. He was quite the oldest man Hawecha had ever seen — more ancient than either Dabassah or Buleh. Seeing her beside him, he began to speak.

"Ah, it is a long, long time since I killed my lion. Today, nobody remembers that! It is now eight years since I was made *gadamoji*. I am the oldest man alive now. Why, I am almost ninety." Far from being depressed at this thought, the old man cackled loudly. "What a life I have had," he continued. "I was a man of great vigour. Now I have seven sons and seventeen grandchildren. I look upon them with pride. These men are still children compared to me." He hobbled off, still cackling.

Before sunset, Hawecha made her way to 'her' trees. She had decided to fast that evening and to pray for inner strength. By sunset, she was ready.

One by one, the women came. When most of the women had assembled — an impressively large crowd — Hawecha cleared her throat.

"We are gathered here for one purpose only: to pray for peace amongst ourselves. I come to you not as Hawecha, a simple woman, but as a peacemaker. That is the will of our high priests. I ask you to pray with me for unity and good character during the days that are to come."

Haltingly at first, but then with firm voice and the power of her convictions, Hawecha led the prayer. Each line she uttered was repeated by the chorus of women. Over and over again, they besought God to assist them. They prayed until their voices failed them. None noticed the bright spangle of the Milky Way that arched above their heads, 'Suleh's pathway' as it was called. Wearily, they tottered to their beds.

# CHAPTER 27

In preparation for their rite of passage, the *gadamoji* had undergone many rituals and purifications. Each one had previously had his hair woven into an upstanding crown about his head.

Around their necks, they wore special necklaces consisting of seeds and one or two thin blue glass rings, bought from their Konso neighbours. Onto each necklace had been carefully stitched a small leather amulet containing hidden magic.

To complete their ceremonial attire, each *gadamoji* had strapped onto his forehead a long, protruding object made of iron or wood which resembled an erect phallus. This was called a *kalacha*.

They had come to Arero from all the surrounding areas. Now that they had gathered together, there were certain rituals which they performed jointly. They also met frequently beneath their special tree to make decisions as to the order of events and how best to carry them out. Meanwhile, each female head-of-household had dug a small hole inside the earth floor of her hut. In this, incense was burned. The women took turns to squat over these holes, thus perfuming and purifying themselves.

On this particular daybreak, the *gadamoji* all withdrew to their anointed tree singing for the last time in their lives a warrior's song. Women and children were forbidden to follow them or witness their prayers. Most of them hid indoors until the elders returned for the morning coffee ritual.

In the neighbouring warren of huts lived a *gadamoji* whose wife was totally blind. Inside the hut, the old wife sat on her stool weeping silently at her helplessness. Hawecha took pity on her and offered to perform the coffee ritual for her.

Two elders sat inside the hut and a third followed behind Hawecha. They exchanged the usual greetings of the morning, and settled down to wait. When the coffee was ready, Hawecha knelt before each elder and asked him to bless the wooden coffee bowl. After each blessing, they chanted in chorus: "*Naga! Naga!*," meaning 'Peace.' It was considered the most important word in their language, next to their name for the Creator.

Hawecha poured the coffee into individual wooden cups and everyone sat around quietly sipping and chewing the beans.

Today was the most important day of the ceremonies. The *gadamoji* would have their elaborate hairstyles shaved off. Their sons would undergo certain initiation rites. One generation would hand over to the other.

Each family had previously selected an animal for sacrifice. Standing by their personal gateway, the family gathered around to bless the animal, stroking it and soothing it. When it was entirely calm, its throat was swiftly cut.

Seven ritual assistants now made their way around the compound checking on the slaughtering. Each carried a special staff of office. They moved from sacrifice to sacrifice, singing and chanting: "We the overseers vouch for the fact that we have seen what there is to see. We are satisfied."

Hawecha stood nearby as her hostess prepared to shave her husband's head. The *gadamoji* sat on a stool beside the slaughtered beast. In front of him, upon the ground, stood a large wooden bowl full of milk and water. He carefully removed the *kalacha* from his forehead and his wife poured over his head a mixture of milk and grass. Using a small, sharp, knife she carefully began to shave and as she did so, his hair, woven into its coronet, fell into the bowl of watery milk.

His son and two male relatives cut strips of skin from the right foreleg of the dead animal and one of these strips was tied around the old man's left wrist. He gave the *kalacha* to his son who was now entitled to wear it. He tied it proudly to a leather band around his forehead.

Hawecha helped the wife to carry the wooden bowl to her *dobbu*. She carefully broke up the coronet and buried both it and her husband's hair in the heap of dung. Gently, she patted the *dobbu* back into shape.

All twenty-two *gadamoji* would now enter a three-day period of seclusion. Her host retired to his hut in order to obey this stricture.

Hawecha was asked if she would like to meet Saar Gindicha, a famous reader of entrails. It was customary to have these read at some point during the ceremony since it was deemed healthy to know the future. Hawecha agreed with alacrity since she was by now most interested in any form of divination.

Saar took a mesenteric membrane from a heap of cow entrails and asked two men to help him hold it up. As they stretched out this 'map' in the air before him, he pointed at this vein and that or at a certain discolouration. Well trained by his father and with many divinations behind him, Saar began to speak.

"There will be many people coming and going through our land soon. They are not enemies, but rather traders. They are Somalis and they bring with them new merchandise. We must make them welcome." He frowned deeply as he studied further. "A war to the north will make them come our way. They will decide to trade with us." He nodded several times before continuing. "There will be war and then peace for a while and then another war. Both will affect our people." He looked up dejectedly and announced that he did not wish to read further.

Those gathered around him sighed deeply. War was part of life. It had been a long time since the last one. Now, Saar predicted *two*, with only a short interval between them. Discouraged, they all turned away.

A crowd of several hundred people gathered outside the compound, lining both sides of the ceremonial gateway. The sons of the *gadamoji* had meanwhile gathered together well outside the village to daub their faces with white clay for which they had bartered. The daughters, their skin and hair well oiled and glistening and each carrying a milk-pot on her back, waited to lead the procession into the houses of their fathers. They represented the future of the tribe since they would eventually bear children.

The seven ritual assistants laid a log across the opening of the gateway to mark the threshold between youth and age. They turned to address the crowd warning them to behave appropriately and to look away as the sons passed through it. Hawecha strained to peer over the heads of those in front of her. The sons drew nearer each with his face painted and showing off his *kalacha*. Hawecha obediently averted her gaze and focused on the ground.

The daughters led the ritual assistants, followed by all the sons, into the house of each *gadamoji* in turn. A large ceremonial milk-pot was untied from the central pole of the hut. The *gadamoji* was required to recite the poem of his life's heroic exploits. As he finished, the milk-pot was seized and removed from the hut.

The procession made its way to the family's animal sacrifice. By now, the meat had been removed for cooking. Only entrails and skin remained. The ritual assistants squatted beside these remnants and took a sip of sour milk from the container. When all seven had sipped, they returned it to the hut from which it had been seized. The remainder of the day was taken up in this dramatic performance, with the procession moving from hut to hut, until all twenty-two *gadamoji* had been properly honoured.

By custom, the women were supposed to gather in groups at night and sing together loudly. Hawecha, pleased that her prayers for peace had worked so well during this eventful and emotional day, decided none were needed now. Better to sing with joy that the holy day had passed without mishap.

Singing was not one of Hawecha's talents; in fact she had been advised to keep quiet on numerous occasions. She stood outside a circle of young women and listened as they raised their voices to the stars, throwing back their heads and giving way to joyous abandon. As they sang, they slapped their feet sharply down upon it providing their own musical accompaniment.

All Hawecha could do was to sway in rhythm. How glorious it must be to sing like them and how she envied them. She realized that God's gifts were many and well-apportioned. Each person had his own. Every human being was important.

The moon rose up, slightly more than a crescent now. She would be there when it was full and again when it began to wane. She had time to build up new friendships. She was comforted by this thought.

# CHAPTER 28

The two families whose sons were to be named had been hard at work extending the rear of their huts to accommodate extra guests.

One of the mothers, Buqqeh, had two nieces to assist her. The second — a friendly woman named Dabbo — was still suckling a baby boy. She asked Hawecha to take care of him between its feedings so that she could relax and get ready.

Her first-born appeared wearing a special leather cap, embroidered with many cowries. He was tall for his age, which Hawecha guessed to be around seven. He was skinny and not particularly handsome. Yet he too might bring lustre to his family tree in time. One day, he too might boast of his exploits.

Dabbo's husband had moved up the social ladder and now occupied a position in the sixth age-set. Dabbo had to move up with him.

A large cowhide was dragged into the open and Dabbo reclined gracefully upon it to have her hair restyled. Until now, she had worn it in the traditional manner of a young mother. The top of her head was braided into many neat plaits, each ending level with her ears. Below this level, her hair was free to spread itself out in a wild bush around her neck. At the back of her head four long iron ornaments had been braided in; two for each of her sons.

An older woman dragged a stool out from the hut and sat down beside Dabbo, ready to create the style now dictated by custom as being suitable for the mother of a son with a name. She un-braided Dabbo's plaits and removed the iron ornaments. These would later be attached to Dabbo's wrist ornament.

Teso now began to re-braid the hair. The new style required a central parting. One by one the new plaits appeared, thicker and therefore fewer than before. At last, Teso grunted in satisfaction and rose to resume other duties. Dabbo got up from her 'couch' and twirled around girlishly. Now everyone could see her status had improved.

Hawecha found the second family nearing the end of their ritual. Both Buqqeh and her husband Waryo wore wide leather bandoliers with many straps across their chests. These were lavishly decorated with many cowries and gourd-tops.

Six months old, first born was held fiercely as he screamed and squalled, while Buqqeh attempted to wash his hair. The two nieces tried to keep him happy by making funny faces. This tactic backfired and the child screamed louder. At last he was thoroughly clean. Sweating profusely, Buqqeh picked him up and made her way to the outer perimeter of their gate.

She had constructed a smaller, oblong mound of cow dung in front of her original *foddu.* These mounds represented the family itself. Now, a new member had been added to it.

Waryo followed her leading a camel by its halter. The nieces loaded two large water-pots onto the camel and tied these down carefully with thongs. Buqqeh held the camel's halter in one hand and a giraffe-hide container full of grass in the other. Buqqeh's aunt was asked to carry the child and Hawecha brought up the rear. Majestically, they stalked back across the compound to their hut.

Now Buqqeh's aunt emptied a little water mixed with milk into a tiny wooden trough that Waryo had carved. Waryo went off to return the camel to its enclosure. When he returned, Buqqeh sat down on a stool outside the hut, poured water onto her son's head and proceeded to shave him. He kicked and screamed and fussed, so that Buqqeh felt unable to continue. Waryo's father stepped in to complete the task with a firm grasp and a no-nonsense approach. The hair fell into the small trough.

Buqqeh's aunt, meanwhile, had collected small branches of bright green leaves which were now planted into the roof of the hut above the doorway. The trough was tucked away amongst them.

Seeing that the complicated rituals were over, Hawecha decided to return to Dabbo. Smiles of welcome greeted her and she was invited to join them after the evening meal.

She realised that yet another evening would pass without a peace-prayer by the women. Should she refuse the naming ceremony and attend to this other matter? She paced up and down, trying to reach a decision. The women had behaved extremely well all day despite their fatigue and the pressures put upon them. By now, they would all be cooking supper and then they would gather to sing again. Surely, they would not quarrel amongst themselves whilst singing? Curiosity won. She would attend the naming.

When she returned, the hut was full of noise. The seven ritual assistants were there as well as many relatives and several guests. Hawecha smiled boldly and gave them all the customary formal greetings before finding a space at the back.

The son sat on a stool towards the rear of the hut. He had had his head shaved and was even uglier in profile than before. Hawecha hoped that life would make a real man of him and give him a character to overcome his physical limitations.

The evening began with a special coffee ritual. Dabbo roasted sixteen coffee beans (eight for each of her sons — eight being the number of years spent in an age-set). The parents each chewed two beans, whilst the remainder were shared out among other relatives or surrogates.

The men broke into a song that told of ancient tribal origins and of the many clans. The song was designed to make the boy a part of his long inheritance and to bind him to the culture. When it was over, a solemn prayer was intoned: long life for the boy and long life for both his parents. The boy was then given his name: Juldess Jillo. It was repeated many, many times.

In the background, Hawecha heard the women begin to sing beneath the stars. Once again, she heard their stomping and clapping. A soprano rose high above the others and words were repeated by a chorus. She too felt a part of her inheritance.

# CHAPTER 29

As she approached Dabbo's hut the following morning, she became aware that the celebrations had lasted all through the night. The ritual assistants were still chanting and singing. She marvelled at how their voices could hold up so long.

Outside the hut a young bull had been slaughtered. A strip of hide had been cut from its belly and Dabbo now wore this across her chest. Two of her husband's brothers were poking long sticks beneath the prone neck of the slaughtered animal, soaking them in the blood that had poured out from its throat. These sticks would become ceremonial sticks for Juldess and his young brother.

Juldess himself was watching all this. Hitherto, he had been treated as a girl. Hawecha wondered what it must be like to suddenly be acknowledged as a member of the male sex. A matter of great pride, she suspected.

Tied around his neck was a carnelian bead. Every now and then his fingers reached up to touch it: smooth and shiny and orange-brown in colour. This bead told the whole world of his new status. Like his mother on the previous day, he delighted in showing off. Several smaller children had gathered around. "I'll smack you if you spoil my ceremony!" he threatened, making a great show of chasing them away. He ran back in time to have a strip of hide tied around his left wrist.

Inside the hut yet another coffee ritual began. When there was no coffee left, Dabbo's husband (whom Hawecha had by now discovered was called Sorah) took down from the roof of the hut the small trough which contained Juldess's hair. He took it to the cattle enclosure and placed it on the back of one his cows which would now form the nucleus of his son's own herd. Sorah knocked the trough off the cow's back so that the hair fell onto the ground. The trough was taken back into the hut and hidden there.

Dabbo, Sorah and other members of the family now made their way to the family *foddu* to collect grass and branches. These were 'planted' at the gateways of their small livestock enclosures and the grass was strewn across the entrances.

Hawecha was left to her own devices. Once more, she sauntered out to the open land that lay to the east of the settlement. She sat down upon a convenient rock and paused to review the events of the past few days.

She had witnessed the rites of passage of three generations: grandfathers, fathers and sons. What a wonderful tradition it was that had devised such an intricate system.

She remembered that all their sages spoke of the First Five Teachers and ran their holy names over and over in her mind: Golo Gobbo, Boru Billo, Maneh Lekha, Babo Galessah and Galeh Anno. She thought of Gadayo Galgallo, who had bequeathed them the age-set system. What enlightened beings they had been!

And her own role? A small one to be sure. Her youth and inexperience were against her. Only one man (albeit a high priest) had faith in her. "Don't let me down," he had instructed. She sighed. Small was better than nothing.

Near to the camel enclosure, she heard sharp voices raised in anger. Two young women were arguing vehemently, all decorum cast to the winds. Hawecha's worst fears had been realised. Women really were such fools, she thought, to let their petty grievances dominate a sacred time like this.

"My husband is higher up in the scale of things than yours is, therefore my wishes come first!" The younger woman stood, head thrown back with out-thrust lower lip, fists clenched at her hips.

"Mrs. High-and-Mighty!" the other taunted. "Just who do you think you are!" she stooped to pick up a handful of dust which she flung into her opponent's eyes. The younger woman hurled herself catlike straight at the older woman's throat. Hawecha knew she had to intervene.

"Stop! Stop this at once!" she shrieked, hoping to be heard. She snatched a nearby branch from its holy position at somebody's cattle entrance and hoped the owner would not mind its new — if lesser — purpose.

Brandishing the branch between the two women's noses, she commanded them to cease. "I am Hawecha. The high priests speak through me. Stop! I command you to stop!" she broke the two women apart. The three of them stood there dishevelled and panting. A large crowd had by now gathered.

Hawecha demanded that the two women ask the men to forgive them for their breach of etiquette. Then she made them apologise to each other in front of all the witnesses. Finally, she commanded the women to pray.

Six stepped forward, Hawecha led them, asking God to forgive them all for their arrogance and childishness. She prayed for peace to be restored and for each woman to examine her heart and conscience and cast out whatever evil lurked there. Hawecha closed her eyes and prayed her heart out.

One by one, other women were drawn in. When exhausted, Hawecha opened her eyes again; she saw that almost the entire female population had gathered around her and that – far to the rear of the female crowd – two of the *gadamoji* had joined in.

Overwhelmed at her success, Hawecha burst into tears. An old lady wrapped both arms around her, then patted down her unkempt hair.

"Well done, my dear. Well done! You live up to your name so well, Hawecha. Come now and sit with me."

She took Hawecha by the hand and led her to her hut, where she pulled up a stool and sat her down. Then she gave her what she most needed: motherly love and comfort.

# CHAPTER 30

The next day marked the emergence of the *gadamoji* from seclusion. As soon as the sun had risen, a sheep was to be slaughtered on behalf of the entire community. The wife of the senior ritual leader held its head in her lap and a spoon full of fat in one hand. People gathered around her. In turn, each woman took a dab of fat from her spoon, daubed it onto the sheep and blessed it. Even tiny babies were involved, carried by their parents and helped to smear on the fat. The sheep stood there calmly, as did the many hundreds of animals still penned up in their enclosures.

One by one the men approached, each carrying the forked stick acquired at his marriage, his rhino-hide whip and a shorter stick. The sheep was killed and its entrails removed and set aside for reading.

"I still see two wars," Saar Gindicha announced. "All our prayers cannot prevent these. However, I feel there will be fewer deaths than I saw originally. Our prayers do help a little." Nods and sighs of relief accompanied this prediction.

"The rain will come — not in abundance — but sufficient for our needs. We must be frugal and husband our next grain crop." More nods and shrugs. Having heard, they dispersed.

Many visitors left now for their own homesteads. Donkeys were loaded up and small caravans departed. Goats and sheep baaed and bleated as they too left in small clouds of dust.

The *gadamoji* gathered beneath their meeting tree in case a final gift was to be brought to them: One goat, one sheep, a handful of tobacco, a small bag of myrrh in honour of the ancestors. All gifts were distributed amongst the community.

The sacred time had ended. From now on, the *gadamoji* would re-enter the world of the profane. They were no longer permitted to carry weapons nor could they act as warriors. They would be regarded as women, addressed by female pronouns.

Hawecha learned of this and found it strange. She had just heard a young boy addressed as a *he* for the first time in his life and now there were old men who had to be called only *she*! It was all extremely puzzling.

Walking around the inside of the enclosure, Hawecha recalled her own vows made at the lawmakers' gathering four years previously. She had promised to teach the women. Surely it was time to begin?

She found her inspiration soon enough. One young woman was doing a very poor job of smoking out her gourd. Another threw out her dirty water right in front of her doorway for all to step on. A third had her hair un-plaited and awry. Hawecha felt her new position entitled her to reprimand them. And so she did, feeling that this was the only way to make progress.

The following day she would give a sewing lesson. She went round begging for spare scraps of leather to work on and for extra cowries.

Three young girls of marriageable age became her first pupils. First, she made sure they knew how to make fine fibre cords to stitch with. She encouraged them to make strong knots so their work would not come undone. Then, painstakingly, she took her iron awl and pierced three pieces of leather with evenly-spaced small holes. Now to sew on the cowries. She taught them her mother's clan pattern: one straight upright; two horizontals, one above the other; two uprights; one horizontal ... and made sure that each girl reached perfection. Nothing else would do.

Time passed as the girls chattered, at first shyly but then with greater confidence. Hawecha thoroughly enjoyed the company of her three 'daughters'. Life could be so sweet at times. This was a time to cherish.

The days spun by in busyness, with little time for introspection. She swept, she cooked and smoked out gourds. She held babies in her arms and rocked them to sleep. She attended to many minor ailments. She awakened automatically with the first light of dawn and cast about for things to teach.

Hawecha knew they all had to conserve water, but there was no excuse for sloppy washing or for women to smell bad 'down there'. Five married women came to her for lessons in basic hygiene.

She was asked to help with a baby who suffered from bouts of severe colic and whose young mother had reached a point of utter exhaustion.

Hawecha realised the baby was being nursed whilst too much anger sat bottled up inside its mother. She taught the mother to pray for peace first and then to suckle her child. The change was little short of miraculous.

Hawecha watched small children as they ran about the village, playing with stones and sticks, giggling and squabbling, jumping up and down in excitement over a large beetle that staggered along its own small pathway, or a green grasshopper that amused them with its antics.

She remembered a game her mother had taught her, and called the children to her. "Who am I? What am I?" she chanted as she pranced around with her two hands held above her head, her index fingers pointing upwards. "I know, I know!" shrieked a little boy. "A dik-dik!" Hawecha paused. She had had in her mind a larger antelope or a Grant's gazelle. But she decided to let him win.

Soon they were all taking turns at being animals. Their attempts at portraying lions or zebras amused her, as did one boy's rolling over and over in the dirt and then trying to somersault in front of them all. It took a long time before Hawecha realised he was pretending to be a dung beetle. She let go of adulthood and rolled upon the ground with him. Other children joined in.

Hawecha had little time to observe the men-folk. They had leather thongs to cut, sandals to repair and livestock to tend to endlessly. Some passed by hurriedly whilst others seemed nervous and over-wrought. Hawecha knew her place. Her work was with the women.

One day, one of the oldest *gadamoji* — formerly known for his taciturnity and greed — came up to her and showed her his new and much kinder nature.

"Well done, girl. We all admire you now. We are too old to help you but it seems you know what to do. May God smile upon you and give you a long life. The women need you badly."

Hawecha was overcome and could not speak. Instead she knelt down in the dust at his feet and kissed the bottom edge of his goatskin. She remained there with head bowed until he had moved off.

# CHAPTER 31

The day of the full moon came round. Hawecha set off on foot with three other women for a nearby village where the long awaited initiations for the first-born would take place. The women sang as they walked, in praise of their men-folk. Hawecha, fortunately for all, kept silent.

There were perhaps ten families in this homestead and thirteen boys were to undergo their initiation. The youngest was a mere six weeks old, whilst the eldest was fourteen or fifteen. No further ceremonies would be performed for two whole years. This one marked the end of a great cycle.

She and her companions were made welcome somewhat hurriedly. The sun would set soon and there was no time for extended politeness. Each was billeted with a different family in order not to overburden anyone. Already, the young boys were being assembled outside the village gate by the man who had offered to lead the ceremony. His name was Boru Waryo and he had brought a special black bull with which to provide food for the villagers.

Some of the boys wore their hair in the long and ragged locks of childhood whilst a few sported a shaven tonsure. All wore goatskins tied over the left shoulder. Each lad carried a short spear, tailor-made to his height, and a short dagger tied to his waist. The father of the baby stood in their midst, showing off his young progeny. The baby also wore a miniature goatskin wrap; he too sported a tiny knife.

Outside the village, the boys sang a song of abuse against the previous generation. Of course *they* would do it all better! A short distance from the gate, a pile of branches had been gathered into which they all planted their short spears. They removed their sandals and scattered in search of firewood which was piled up to the left of the gate, under instruction from Boru. They then entered the village and were given water to drink as the reward for all their labour.

A large branch was dragged in front of the gate. The boys gathered around it and sang a song in praise of all the clans. The older boys deepened their voices as far as they could and shuddered as they chanted. Their fathers joined in with lower, deeper voices.

Now the cattle could be seen returning from their grazing. As the cows entered the village, each boy collected his spear and some of the firewood and filed in behind the livestock. The gateway was closed in with branches for the night. The boys entered the cattle pen, walked around it once and then made their way towards their special hut, one large enough for all of them. The seven eldest were chosen to be the leaders and two more were elected as helpers. Nine spears were planted in the ground just outside the doorway.

Women came bearing small gifts of salt or tobacco. The boys tied these up into a corner of their wraps. Other women approached, bringing milk for them to drink. When they had drunk their fill, everyone returned to the cattle pen, where Boru Waryo waited with his black bull.

The boys gathered around the bull, placed their hands upon it and sang a song with a slow and calming rhythm. Boru stroked its back with his forked stick. It sank slowly to the ground, of its own free will, head bowed in submission. Its throat was slit, skin flayed and several elders withdrew the entrails and proceeded to read them. "A lucky day! A long life for all the boys," one pronounced, pointing excitedly at something only he could see. Three heads nodded in agreement. "Healthy minds, these boys have," a second announced. The future seemed particularly rosy.

Hawecha longed to read the entrails also, feeling intuitively that she could. But unless invited to do so, she — like the bull — had to submit.

Eventually, the meat was roasted and all partook of a meal. Fingers dug into large wooden pots, pulling out fatty morsels. Bones were chewed upon and then tossed to the village dogs and chins were smeared with grease. Somebody belched loudly. It seemed a fitting ending.

# CHAPTER 32

Hawecha left the settlement and returned to her own home. She was surprised to find herself morose and without a sense of purpose. After all her great and unexpected successes, this was perhaps unsurprising; there is often a let-down after exaltation. Yet Hawecha had expected to carry all her new-found strength in her heart for ever. She had thought it would sustain her. Now she found the reality of mundane life almost insupportable. Everybody knew her and there were no challenges or thrills.

Certainly, the villagers came to her with their complaints still. She was shown utmost respect and obedience. Yet there was no companion, confidante or friend. She had risen to the heights and now she sensed only her mortality and loneliness. Her emotions overwhelmed her. Above all, she longed for somebody to talk to. She had been the Chosen One. She had given and given and given of herself, until she had nothing more to give. Now she wanted to be cherished.

After a period of listlessness, while she pondered deeply on her state of woe and chewed frequently on her lower lip, she realised that she had to find a friend. She was not ready to while away endless hours gazing into the flames of her fire.

She surveyed the younger women in the village. There were roughly twenty of them, all married of course, and without exception all busily involved with the lives of their children. It seemed impossible that any one of these would find time for her; to chat and gossip idly.

She made her way down to the river in the early morning. Six of these young women were there. She knew them all: there was Godanna-The-Basket-Maker, brash and bold and a bit too reminiscent of the Godanna who had stolen her husband; her younger sister Bonsa-Know-It-All was (as her name implied) not of a particularly sensitive nature; Dabbo-The-Beauty who had not enough intellect for Hawecha's needs; Dhaki-The-

Careless, although well-intentioned, broke or lost everything that came her way; Sakeh-The-Golden who had a sunny nature which inspired everyone to be happier, but also had a somewhat malicious tongue. Lastly, there was Khalloh-The-Needy, with deep frown lines between her eyes and a mouth turned downwards by her prolonged sorrows.

Hawecha realised her companion had to come from this group or not at all. The other women had too many children to allow for free time spent in idleness. She cast her mind upon them once again. All had their backs turned to her, as they performed their ablutions, so none was aware of her. She studied their auras carefully hoping for further insights.

Bonsa would give her good advice, Khalloh would never let her down and Sakeh would cheer her up. These three would improve life for her even if only for a single day. She plunged in up to her waist and joined them.

It was not as difficult as she supposed nor was it a matter of 'coming down to their level'. The water was, at this particular time, deep and soothing, cool and refreshing. The women splashed about quite happily, extending the hour of cleanliness as long as they possibly could. They were pleased to see Hawecha and asked her to come again.

Her hour at the river became a daily pastime. After a week, she smiled. The next day, she laughed. Then one day she made a silly joke and they *all* laughed. Sakeh invited her to join the family at its evening meal and Hawecha accepted. She became an adopted aunt to Gayo and Barracho, two exuberant small boys.

Khalloh spoke to her of her husband's inability to breed goats, trade well, or to produce a healthy crop. He preferred to whittle away at small sticks all day lost in a daydream of his own. The family was poor and was endlessly begging and borrowing. Khalloh confided to Hawecha that her husband was almost always inattentive and careless but she loved him too much to breathe a word of his deficiencies. Since he was a kind man and clearly loved Khalloh equally, Hawecha swore to keep the family secret.

Gradually — almost imperceptibly — she felt herself drawn in to village life in ways not open to her before. Had she held herself aloof before? Or were they different now? In the end it mattered not. She realised it was not sufficient to be their healer; she had to be approachable. She had to care more.

Her compassionate side developed rapidly. Each day, she would ask herself, "who needs me?" or "what can I do to make somebody else's life better?" Slowly, she came out of her self-centred introspection.

One day, she looked directly into Sakeh's eyes and saw real love for her reflected there. For Hawecha, this represented a triumph. Deeply moved, she made sure she returned it in countless little ways.

# CHAPTER 33

Hawecha awakened screaming and sat up panting on her pallet. Then she understood that the screams were all inside her, still emerging from the top of her head.

The Dream had been ugly, horrible and terrifying. First, she had seen three children writhing in agony and then dying. She saw great scabs upon their arms and legs and across their skinny bellies. Their wasted bodies lay stretched out before her, one next to the other. Her inner eye had then seen a mother looking at her arm in horror, as the skin peeled off entirely exposing bare bones beneath.

As if this were not sufficiently nightmarish, her father's ghost had risen before her screaming "Go! Go!" in a voice that was not his. It seemed to bleat like a goat's and then bellow like that of a wild, fierce bull. Her mind had leapt to the millet fields, seeing them scorched and flattened. The ground lurched before her and rose as if to walk away. She sat there gasping for breath. Not since her early childhood has she dreamed as vividly as this.

She got up and paced about her small hut, tripping and stumbling in the darkness. Light. She needed a ray of light. Shivering uncontrollably, she managed to blow upon her embers, to set a little kindling to them, and — at last — to dissipate the gloom of both inner and outer world.

"Suleh, help me! Help me!" she murmured, rocking back and forth upon her haunches. "Sirius, comfort me. Oh, Sirius, walk by my side."

She sensed a slight shift in the atmosphere about her and then a kind of shimmering. Suleh spoke to her then. "Honour your dream, Hawecha. It is a predictive one. God has shown you the future. You must, you must obey. Only *you* can save the villagers from the horrors you have been shown. It is your work, Hawecha. Please listen!"

The voice of Suleh faded; the shimmer seemed to transform itself into the voice of Sirius. She sensed red light around her. "Hawecha, dream no more for the prediction may become reality. You must take the dream into your heart, and understand why it has come to you. Obey the Laws of God. Obey and all will go well. Obey, Hawecha. Obey!"

The hut seemed to shake with the power of this last word. A shaft of violet light invisible to all but Hawecha, came down to earth from heaven, piercing the top of her head and easing her agitated breathing. She sensed that it had come from God.

"Study the dream again!" came her instructions.

She recalled the children moaning, sweating and dying. A high fever was clearly indicated as the source. Again, she saw the scabs: now they suppurated horribly. And the bare bones. The disease would bring a ghastly, painful death. Hawecha shuddered violently.

And the fields of millet? Scorched and flattened. How well she remembered those — identical to the fields of her childhood dreams — when the people would not listen. She recalled her father's voice telling her to go. Holy One, Great God where to? The answer came. "To the west, Hawecha. Lead the people westwards. Some may still die from the terrors you have seen, but not as many as if you do nothing. They know how serious you are. This time they will listen."

Hawecha scratched herself, already feeling the itch of whatever it was that would kill them all. She felt the hot sun that would deprive them of food burn through her very marrow. Disease and famine. The end of all her people!

"Not so," Suleh whispered. "You have been given a prophetic dream. Go, and prophecy!"

Hawecha felt contained and trapped inside her hut. She walked about agitatedly outside. Still, she felt the need for more space around her. She dragged the branches from the village gateway so that she could pass through and carefully pulled them back in place behind her, leaving the villagers protected for what remained of the night.

How many nights could they sleep there in peace and ignorance? An inner voice replied: "only three." She had only three nights in which to speak.

Outside, a half-moon appeared from behind a cloud. "Half this and half other." Hawecha moaned. "What kind of omen is that?" she came close to cursing God.

A puff of wind surprised her, died down and then flared up again. "That's not an omen. I can't make anything out of wind!" Round and round in circles Hawecha paced and stumbled, looking for succour. Her hair awry and near-madness in her eyes, Hawecha decided to speak at once. To prolong her own agony was impossible. Unthinkable!

As dawn broke, a distraught Hawecha pounded on the doorway of the spiritual leader. Harero had long since died. It was his son — himself a man of venerable years — who hollered from within and at length emerged to see her. Before him, Hawecha wrung her hands and stammered out apologies. One look and Doyo knew calamity had befallen.

Hawecha explained her Great Dream to him, mustering a little more courage and greater eloquence as he questioned her. "May I call the villagers together at once, Father?" she pleaded. He was thrown into confusion and asked for time to pray. Hawecha returned to her hut, knowing he would call on her when he was ready.

Some form of purification seemed in order. Glad to have found an occupation, Hawecha scooped out the mud floor of her hut forming a shallow bowl. She took a lump of myrrh from a pouch, lit it with an ember and squatted over the aromatic resin.

She thought of her mother and innumerable other women who had purified themselves in the same fashion. Once more, generations of customary usage brought her a degree of comfort. Later, she swallowed a few mouthfuls of gruel. Hawecha felt able to proceed.

Doyo came to her door. "I saw in your eyes that you were fearful. I also saw that you were honest. I prayed for courage to play my own part. God told me to obey. I will call the people together, but it is *your* Dream. Therefore, *you* must explain it."

Hawecha followed him to his hut where he collected his forked stick so all would know he had assumed an official role. He went to each doorway in turn asking the occupants to meet beneath the holy tree. There was no time for explanations.

When the crowd had gathered, he stood up to address them calling upon his ancestors to bear witness to the fact that he had prayed long and hard before disturbing them. He pushed Hawecha to the fore and sat down upon a tree-root, bowing his head in submission.

Hawecha spoke long and well, reiterating the salient points of her vision: the fever, the scabs, the bare bones, the dead children, the fields of no millet and her father's voice; then Suleh's guidance and that of Sirius. And at the end, the voice of God. They must move in order to evade disaster. They must pack up and move to the west.

Her words fell upon a palpable silence. She could sense the fear. She could see each aura shrink and turn grey and cold. She faced a crowd of fear and cold.

By evening, it had been decided that those who believed would leave in two days. Each family retired to its home to face manifold decisions. To go or to remain and defy destiny? To meet death in familiar surroundings, or to settle elsewhere? Amongst strangers? Or with relatives? With the others ... or should they fend for themselves? To take, or do without?

In the morning, those who had decided to leave began to pack up. Hawecha made the rounds of the village to see who had decided what.

Khalloh and Sakeh were staying. The ritual leader had decided to remain. The blows fell upon Hawecha's head one by one. Only half would go. She had done her utmost; half was better than none.

Only the future would show who had been right and who had not. And what was 'right' in any case? Death had to be faced one day. Sooner or later. That was the only choice for some. She herself would move. Guided from above, Hawecha would find a good place.

# CHAPTER 34

What a sorry caravan they formed as they accompanied Hawecha on their journey westwards. Barracho took the lead since it was unseemly for a woman to do so. Beside him strode his young wife Dhaki. Upon their donkey was strapped a new-born son and a boy of two struggled to keep pace on foot. He was 'divided up' amongst the other beasts of burden whenever he felt tired.

In the middle were other donkeys, heavily laden. Some of their burdens slipped sideways and had to be re-arranged from time to time. Doyo, Borou and Gayo volunteered to look after them leaving their wives to manage several small children. There were amongst their number only two girls of marriageable age. Both walked dolefully beside their parents.

Bringing up the rear came a young stalwart named Jarso, yet unmarried. Since they were all of the same clan, marriage between him and either of the two young girls was quite unthinkable. All three would have to wait until they could form exogamous relationships.

Djilloh led the communal herd of goats assisted by two young lads. Arero was ailing and sat upon his donkey with bowed head and a fever upon him. His wife Rufo walked beside him, stopping for frequent rests. She was in her sixth month of pregnancy; brave woman. They were glad to stop for her.

Nobody spoke. It seemed everything had already been said. Each mourned the loved ones left behind — perhaps never to be seen again.

They passed by one village after several low hills had been traversed. Hawecha felt they should spend the night there since it was beginning to grow colder and she hoped there would be room for them all. Barracho volunteered to ask as they waited outside the gate. He emerged shaking his head. "They can take only six of us." He turned to Hawecha and asked what they should do. She felt they should not divide themselves up any further. If they crowded around the beasts for warmth, surely they could camp together beneath the stars? Reluctantly, all agreed.

One by one, small fires were lit and evening meals prepared. Hawecha boiled up a potion for Arero and settled him down on the ground beside her. The goats were 'penned' inside a human circle. Hawecha went to talk to hers as she did every night. All was well with them. The baby fell asleep contentedly — the only one of them at peace.

"How far is it, Hawecha?" asked one of the small boys.

She could only shake her head in shame for indeed, she did not know. 'West' could be very far indeed. She prayed for some sort of clarification.

"Two days more for some of you. Others can rest tomorrow." She brightened up and told him he would soon sleep beneath a roof again. He went off to advise his mother.

One by one, the exiles settled down to slumber. Only Hawecha could not find relief. They were her responsibility. The burden weighed heavily upon her.

In the morning, they all awoke before dawn shivering and hopping about for warmth. After a taste of hastily-prepared gruel, they loaded up once more and resumed their journey. The goats seemed happy, Hawecha noticed and the children smiled today. Perhaps it would not be so terribly sad after all.

Morning turned to noon and noon to early evening, yet no village did they pass. Again, they settled down to their makeshift campsite with only the stars as a roof above their heads. Towards midnight, Arero died; his fever had risen far beyond any medicament Hawecha could provide.

The men-folk rose in the dark at her behest, to bury him immediately. She was afraid the corpse would be taken away by hyenas, lions or other predators. What a sad ending. Well, one had found rest, just as God had foretold.

A shriek awakened her before dawn. One of the small boys had been bitten by a snake. Hawecha bound the wound up tightly, wishing Dabassah were there to advise her. The arm puffed up and turned blue. Within an hour, little Waryo was dead. A second grave was dug.

Another day passed in mournful silence. Another night was spent under the vaults of heaven. They huddled together as best they could, tightening their circle.

By noon of the following day, a village could be seen in the distance, large and well constructed, with millet fields not far off. Their spirits rose as they approached. The news was good. All could stay the night but not all could settle permanently. Would they like to build their own village nearby? Many willing hands would assist them in establishing themselves. The offer was alluring.

After much discussion and a good meal inside the warm huts, it was agreed upon. Now, a future lay before them. Now, each one could catch up on sleep. Hawecha, too worn out to fret, fell into a deep, untroubled slumber awakening long after dawn had broken.

# CHAPTER 35

In the morning, Hawecha presented herself to the ritual leader, in order to explain more fully the reasons for the hasty departure from her village. Jarso-the-wise listened courteously, but she could see disbelief written in his eyes. "Never mind. Never mind," he muttered. "You are all here now. You had best begin your new life at once!"

Thus summarily dismissed, Hawecha suggested to Barracho that they at once select a suitable location for their homestead. The two of them paced about to select the ideal site. The river ran deep here unlikely to dry up so easily. A low range of hills lay behind them. In front, a wide and flat land stretched until the next range of low hills. It looked friendly and promising.

Hawecha made her way to a tall tree and decided her hut would sit beneath it. The doorway would face westwards — with its back to her original home. She never wanted to see that again, she determined. The others would plan for themselves.

Seemingly overnight, the huts sprang up: one here, one there, two together, another one apart. Rapidly, the all-enclosing thorn hedge was created, with one entrance for each family.

They planted their seeds near the riverbank, watered them well and waited for the first crop. Meanwhile, an arrangement was made with Jarso's people. They would provide millet for now, in return for half the eventual harvest. Hawecha realised they would have to be thrifty and eat frugally until the next rains came.

Now that they were settled, they waited for news. Hawecha's insides were continually knotted. What if she were proved wrong? More importantly, what if her vision was accurate? She could not decide which outcome would be preferable; both were equally disastrous.

Six weeks later, they heard. Harkalo stumbled into their village, his eyes wide and staring with shock. He was the sole survivor. The disease had struck quite suddenly, with Sakeh as its first victim. She had developed sores on her arms and legs and died of a great fever. Hawecha shook with anguish. Her best friend had gone. No longer would Sakeh's tongue make its snide remarks. Oh, what Hawecha would give for a sharp retort or a brutal reprimand. Better that than this annihilation!

Two children had succumbed next, crying piteously in the night. The scourge had taken them all, all but this one lad, who, unable to bear the solitude, (as indeed who could?) had picked up their trail and followed them. He had simply faced the setting sun and walked directly towards it.

He collapsed into Hawecha's arms sobbing and moaning with all the pent up emotion of his shock. Why had he escaped the scourge? Why was *he* so strong? Hawecha told him he had come as her messenger, to confirm her prophecy. She gave him what comfort she could and took him in to live with her until he had recovered from his nightmare.

Now all of them were afraid, including Jarso and his whole village. If the pestilence had come, then next would come the famine. Anxiously, they scanned the horizon daily seeking large dustclouds or some other evil omen.

Instead, a gentle rain fell upon them. The new seedlings sprouted. They grew. A good crop was predicted.

Behind them to the east, however, a different weather pattern had manifested. Between their range of hills and those they had left behind them, a drought cut a sweeping path. It took months for all the news to reach them. What the sun had not destroyed, a swarm of locusts had taken. Hawecha had seen this dark cloud as it swept in from the north — a great swathe of black in the sky. Locusts leave nothing behind them. Those who had not been cut down by the pestilence had ultimately died of hunger.

Nobody knew how many had perished. But each family present could estimate its personal losses. The women knelt and wept. The village mourned for their friends and relatives. They prayed for calm and strength. They prayed for a new life amongst new friends. They prayed for another clan to send its youth towards them so new marriages could take place. They prayed for health and children.

When Rufo gave birth to a healthy son, both villages rejoiced. It was the first new spark of life for them all. At last — a joyous omen!

# CHAPTER 36

One day, many months later, Hawecha was collecting herbal remedies with which to replenish her stock. She had climbed half way up the hillside and now the sun was hot, too hot for arduous work. She decided to nap under a thornbush until the worst was over.

When she awakened, she was surprised to find only one thought in her head: Mount Abunu! She had heard from Dabassah many years ago of the Oromo sacred mountain but had given it little thought since then. She would go there. With this idea firmly planted, she strode down the hillside carrying her small bundles and singing raucously to the wind. After all, the wind could bear her poor voice. Her heart had to rejoice somehow.

She made suitable arrangements for somebody else to tend her goats – now multiplied to eighteen. Then she loaded her necessities onto her donkey and prepared to set off. "Are you never happy in one place?" Barracho asked petulantly. "Why must you always roam about?" Barracho had a point: after all, she was there to heal them should they fall ill. Hawecha explained that she had to go wherever her heart (or God) called her. "I have work to do. Sometimes, I need a rest from it!" She stormed off, refusing further discussion.

The way was long and harder than expected. She, who had grown accustomed to a fast pace and to shrugging her shoulders against adversity, now struggled over stony ground. The soil had greatly eroded in places; her path now took her up and down steep ravines. From time to time, she backtracked seeking an easier way. She never gave up! Day after day she awoke with the dawn, faced the sun's glory and headed directly towards it. One day, she would reach her destination.

A week later, she was close. She had come across two goatherds who had informed her the sacred mountain lay just over the next range of hills. On she struggled, propelled by inner purpose. At last, panting and gasping, she stood atop the hills surveying the vast panorama before her.

A little to the left Mount Abunu reared its proud head. Hawecha was somewhat disappointed. She had expected a peak of vast proportions, completely blocking out the horizon. Mount Abunu was more rounded and far smaller than she had envisioned. Nonetheless, it was the highest point for as far as she could see. She understood why it had been declared holy. Even from where she stood, it had an aura about it. Yes, even a mountain had an aura, Hawecha realised. This one was truly enormous, red and gold and a colour new to her. Having nothing in nature with which to compare it, she had no means whereby to describe or define it. She shrugged — a by-now-habitual response — and made her way towards the mountain.

More difficult than she had supposed, for there was no direct routing. She twisted and turned around scattered boulders, leading her poor donkey over rough clods of earth and through tangled bushes. Wait-a-bit thorns clutched at her arms and legs; once, she had to pause to untangle her hair. Now she stood on level ground. Ahead, she could see tall trees strung out in one long line — clearly demarcating the banks of a substantial river.

Upon reaching it, she found it too deep to cross. She spent a whole day searching for signs of habitation and finally came upon a small village.

They had heard of her! It seemed Hawecha was by now famous. "Pity it took so many horrible deaths to make me known," she thought, as blessings were heaped upon her. The women vied with each other to feed and house her.

In the end, she decided to stay with the eldest. Nobody could quarrel with that. Everyone wanted to hear the story of her life. Guilt plucked at her heart when they asked her to stay on.

"Thank you, but I must go back to my family. I brought them out of danger. I must stay there now."

Replete, warm and heartened by their reception and her new-found recognition, she sat by the old woman's fire and watched its light dwindle gradually. They had called her Hawecha-The-Prophetess.

She basked in her new-found title.

# CHAPTER 37

Two days later, Hawecha marched with renewed vigour towards the mountain. She felt it improper to have her donkey accompany her on a pilgrimage and had left it behind in the village. Over her shoulder she had slung a large bag containing an extra goatskin, her sandals and sufficient dried goat meat for three days. Also over her shoulder hung a gourd full of water. She had forded the river at a shallower place in an ox-bow bend. Now nothing lay between her and Mount Abunu.

The incline was far steeper than she had supposed and Hawecha had to pause for breath every minute, it seemed. She was exasperated with her slow progress, Mount Abunu being higher than she had thought. She slipped and slithered upwards, sending showers of small stones down the slopes behind her. Hawecha had never climbed a mountain and at that point she decided that never again would she do so.

By late afternoon she had scaled the last crags. Now she stood on the top, with all the north before her, her breath becoming calmer and stronger, while she surveyed this new land. Flat plains stretched far into the horizon: the widest space she had ever seen. Not as beautiful somehow as the land with which she was familiar, the southern regions behind her. *Her* part of Liban was by far the best, she felt. A wave of homesickness overwhelmed her. Too late for regrets. She suppressed her feelings hastily.

She sat down upon a rock and closed her eyes. At once, she became aware of a change in the atmosphere. From her rock to a small hillock in the distance, she could 'see' a pale blue line, the colour of the forget-me-nots that sprang up along the pathways after rain. The line was straight as an arrow: it shimmered in the air. "Made by God," she understood, "to link one sacred place with another." Another passed right through her, originating at some invisible point far to the north-west and stretching for an unimaginable distance behind her to the south-east. "To another holy place," Hawecha realised.

Her pilgrimage had begun well, with new knowledge given. Hawecha stood and stretched her arms up to heaven, both to ease her aching muscles and to try to reach up to God.

"What do you want of me, Creator of us all? I feel very small today. Please tell me what to do next, how to do it and when. I have come from far, far away. Tell me how to go home again and how to help my people."

As always, with calm and complete surrender of her ego, the answers came. "Teach the people, Hawecha. Teach cleanliness and fine stitches, behaviour, prayers and stories. You know far more than you think. Entertain them with stories of the forebears. All of them will listen. Some will be inspired just as you were. Pass the knowledge on."

For two nights and one day, Hawecha remained there in total isolation receiving further insights. On the second night, she prayed for her ancestors to visit her and help her through her vigil.

The spirit of her father came at once, advising her to be patient. He told her he was in excellent health and indeed, she could see this for herself, for he stood before her young and strong again. He explained that where he lived was green and pleasant. He had many, many cattle. He pointed behind him to show her these. She could make out many large, curved horns and many humps as high as small mountains. She could hear their gentle mowing. She sighed with relief: all was well up there.

Later, her mother came in spirit, smiling and holding out her arms. In one hand she held a flower — one not known to Hawecha. White and small and many-petalled. It smelled so sweet!

"Keep it in your heart, Hawecha. I cannot leave it with you. It can only grow up here."

Behind her mother came her mother's mother, Ayo Midadu, the Beautiful One — the one who had also taught. Hawecha had only heard of her. How stately she was, how graceful and how perfect was her profile. The spectre came much nearer, smiling pleasantly.

"They say you are like me, child. But I feel you are better than I was. My beauty complicated my vocation. I was always aware of my body. You are pretty without great beauty and kept in your place more than

I was. I like you, child. One day, up here, you can visit me and we will talk. I know those blue lines that you have been contemplating. Up here, I have learned much more."

Her father returned briefly, counselling her to obey ancient custom and find a worthy person to whom to pass on all her knowledge. "A young woman would be best," he added. "You will recognize her by the blue around her head."

Thus passed the second night with friends from the afterworld to keep her company. Hitherto, she had only dreamed of them yet now they came to her as she sat there, fully conscious. Truly, there was no such thing as death, Hawecha saw. The shades lived in their world but could communicate with those on earth quite easily. Perhaps one only had to ask.

As the sun rose, casting a rosy glow upon her world, Hawecha ate the last morsels of meat, tasty and fatty. A feeling of satisfaction took hold of her. She was loved and now respected. God had given her more work. She still felt fairly young (although all of her age-mates were by now mothers and one or two even grandmothers). Old age could wait awhile.

Down below, in the village, she had been introduced to a woman of still-sharp mind, who — judging by her memories and the number of *gadamoji* ceremonies she had attended — was said to be an octogenarian. Compared to her, Hawecha was very young indeed. She would push old age aside forever.

It was with such encouraging thoughts that Hawecha returned to the village, two days later — having explained over and over again that it was inappropriate to discuss what had taken place on the holy mountain; that what had occurred was for her alone; that no, she had no prophecy for them.

Hawecha bade them all farewell and faced the long journey homewards. Her pilgrimage was over.

# CHAPTER 38

On returning to her home, Hawecha's first thoughts concerned passing her knowledge on in accordance with her father's instructions. She studied the villagers one by one. "Too flighty and her aura is rather grey." Another was pink, not blue. "Too harsh." One young woman had a bluish aura, but she also manifested a quick temper which flared up as dirty orange. Disappointed, Hawecha cast her net wider and studied visitors to the two villages. For a time, nobody seemed suitable.

After several weeks when Hawecha had reached a point of despair, a young unmarried girl came to stay with her cousins and help with a new baby. Her head was swathed in blue light. Nimble fingers, a keen mind and an agile body completed the picture. Hawecha rejoiced and offered to teach the girl herbal medicine — a practical beginning.

For several weeks Dhaki-The-Nimble followed Hawecha on her expeditions squatting down beside her mentor feeling, smelling and sensing whichever plant Hawecha had found. She proved to be a perfectionist and avid for more information. Hawecha watched proudly as she supervised Dhaki's first decoction and felt her own aura glow bright red.

One day, Dhaki did not appear as she usually did at mid-morning. Hawecha paced anxiously outside her hut and finally made her way to the hut were Dhaki lived with her cousins.

"She awakened feeling weak and feverish. I was just coming to tell you," Taditi announced.

At once, Hawecha began her ministrations. Sweats, cramps, then violent diarrhoea. As the day lengthened, the symptoms increased and so did Hawecha's work. Through the night she nursed her pupil.

By morning, Dhaki was no better. Hawecha mustered three young girls to fetch a continuous supply of water with which to bathe poor Dhaki's body. The fever rose and rose. By late afternoon, to touch Dhaki was like touching a live coal.

There came a spasm; the body turned rigid. A moan. A small sigh. The sphincter released a foul and blackish eruption. Dhaki's short life was over.

Hawecha ran outside the compound pulling madly at her hair. She ran far out into the savannah until she had no more breath, stumbling over roots and rocks, her arms torn to shreds by the waiting thorns. Then she raised her arms to heaven and railed at God with all the pain of bereavement.

"How could you do this to me?" she screamed. "I had only just begun!"

She stooped to pick up a handful of dirt and threw this "into God's face". Then she kicked at the ground until her foot bled. Oblivious to the pain, she continued her wild ranting.

"I will not look for another pupil, God," she sobbed. "I have no more heart left for it." In the midst of her agony, the solution came. "I will teach many, not one. You will have to make do with that."

Having vented her spleen, she stalked back to the compound.

When she had regained her composure and when the settlement had recovered from this latest loss, Hawecha began her new mission. She felt it appropriate to teach the villagers from the very beginning — from the history of the creation of their world. She gathered the small children of both villages around her, took up a stout stick with which to threaten them should they prove inattentive and without preamble, began.

"First, there was God, all-powerful and all-knowing. Stronger than any of us." The children wriggled about to make themselves more comfortable. A story could last forever!

"Not a story," Hawecha had said. This was real fact.

"God came first and then God made the world one thing at a time. The first thing that God created was water. Not a river that moves about: just a lump of water." Hawecha could see the water, but describing it was surprisingly difficult. It was simply a creation without shape or form. Yet, for small children, she felt they had to understand it. Symbols from their world would have to come to help her.

"This lump of water was made in two places at the same time." She showed them her two clenched fists by way of illustration. All the little ones obediently emulated her, feeling the lumps of water.

Hawecha laughed. She recognized that her own healing process had begun. She remembered how enthralled she herself had been as a small child, hearing these great tales. Success lay entirely in the hands of the narrator. She would outdo herself to entertain them. She would give them the history, but also the *feel* of it.

"The water was made in two places at the same time." One of her clenched fists reached upwards, as she thrust the other down towards the ground. The children nodded. They could see two places easily. "The lower place was our Earth," she elucidated further, making sure even the littlest one would know it was their world that had just been made. "Neither of these places was solid and hard in those days." She stamped her feet to indicate what solid was. "Both those worlds were made of air." Air was explained adequately as what you breathed in and out each moment of your life. Hawecha felt her imagery had been well understood.

"With some of this water up here," she indicated her upper fist, "Great God made our first star: our beloved Sirius. You all know it. If you look up in the sky at night, it is the biggest and brightest star. You can't miss it!"

The older children nodded in agreement showing off their superiority; they had learned of Sirius long ago. Hawecha lowered her hands to her lap, having ensured that the existence of the first star was well and truly understood.

"Next, God took some of the water from earth and used it to make the sky." She pointed upwards to the blue and white of it, with great feathers of clouds reaching upwards, to emphasise the vastness. "Then, earth was made solid and hard, just as it is now."

The children were by now mesmerised. She looked around the small crowd of twenty or so upturned faces. Some were still chubby with childhood whilst a few were already thinning out into pre-puberty. She wandered what the future held in store for each child present. Would any be inspired?

"From all these things God had already made — from water, air, Sirius, the earth and that other world up there — from these five things, God then made the things we know of here. He made big trees for us to sit under. He made rivers for us to wash in. He made wells in the earth for us to drink from when the rivers have gone. He made cows, goats, camels and sheep. He made a very full world for us, with all the things we would need. At last, God made us. You know, people! Men, women and children. It all began with one man. His name was Taboh."

She paused and asked them to repeat this name. It was the name of 'Everybody's Great-Great-Grandfather.' She wanted to make sure they could all say it. A chorus of loud 'Tabohs' made it quite clear that they all could. "Taboh was different from all other men. He lived in a land called Egypt. At once a chorus of 'Egypt' informed her they were still listening. He lived there all by himself. He was a prophet."

Hawecha paused to emphasise the next point since it was a truly extraordinary one. "Taboh lived by himself for eight hundred years — more years than we will ever see. If you added all our years up one by one — yours and mine and everyone in our two villages — there would still not be enough. That is how long Taboh lived.

One day, somewhere in the middle of those years, God sent Taboh a wife. She was called Tababoh." Without a pause, the children repeated loudly the name of 'Everybody's Great-Great-Grandmother.' "They lived together for a thousand years more than each of them had lived separately and then one day, Tababoh had a baby boy. They called him Wayu Taboh." Again, the name was repeated. "When Wayu Taboh was one hundred years old — not so very, very old — his father Taboh died."

The smaller children shrieked and had to be cuddled by the older ones. It took some time before peace was restored. Hawecha digressed from her story to remind them that death had to come to all one day, even to the greatest hero, even to their most illustrious ancestors. Yes, even to her. The story took on a sad note until she could resume it.

"Luckily, Tababoh was already pregnant and soon gave birth to a very healthy daughter."

They were delighted at this turn of events and clapped and cheered the little girl — whose name, it transpired, was Masuleh. Her name was repeated very loudly indeed, so happy were they all to have the generations continue.

"Both Wayu Taboh and Masuleh lived for many years with their mother Tababoh. When they were both completely grown up, they married each other. Together they made a son whom they called Banoh." The son's name was now repeated for posterity.

Remembering what Dabassah had pointed out to her as being of supreme importance, Hawecha explained that in the ancient language of the Oromo, words were very different from the one's they used now. The word *banoh* meant "a way in" — which she likened to going into a hut through its opening. That opening was a *banoh* in the old days.

"After a long time, Masuleh gave birth to her second child — this time a daughter. Her name was Manoh." There were more girls than boys in her audience. The female names resounded more loudly than those of the males. Hawecha noticed this. "Already history is being bent a little, without any assistance from me," she remarked wryly to herself, before returning to 'the facts'.

"After many years, Banoh married his sister Manoh." Hawecha raised her head to look about her for now she had come to the whole point of this long and colourful dissertation. The children looked back at her waiting. "Good, I have held their attention all this long time," Hawecha thought. "Either they are very good children ... or I am an excellent story-teller."

"The point of all these names I have given you is that *all* the children of the whole wide world are descended from Banoh and Manoh. Banoh was, as I have said, the way in. The way in to what? To all the generations. To your grandfathers and grandmothers, some of whom are still alive. To your parents — long may they live. And now, at last, to all of you who sit before me! Isn't that astonishing?" Indeed it was.

Hawecha had found a role she truly loved. She would have to tell more stories.

# CHAPTER 39

Now that Hawecha was famous, people came from other villages, sometimes travelling two days to reach her. The word had spread that she could see 'everything'. Hawecha, who knew that she could not, prayed nightly for help from above, through whatever she could not handle herself.

Her fame as a story-teller also spread and some of her patients brought their children with them, specifically to learn of the 'old days.'

Hawecha delved and dug into her own past under Dabassah's tutelage, dredging up whatever memories lay buried there. She found a few episodes in Oromo history that inspired her. Gathering the children around her — sometimes three and sometimes twenty — she would teach whatever had popped into her head the night before.

She told them of Habba Noyeh, the Somali queen, who had so angered the men-folk that they had ended her reign by luring her into a deep pit and spearing her to death. That tale was meant as an admonition to the girls in her audience not to overstep their powers. It proved to be extremely popular.

For the boys, she had another story, the life of one of their great heroes: Abbayi Babo. He had been the leader of an eight-year age-set, the 'Father of an Era'. He had brought together all the surrounding tribes to live peacefully and follow the same laws. Only the Warda people had refused. Eventually, by various subterfuges and ruses, he had won them over.

Once she had pleased them with these morsels of ancient history, she was able to return to more spiritual subjects. She taught them about Sofmari, a great mystic who was still with them — in charge of their spiritual lives. He had found a great cave with many subterranean passages leading to and from it. There he had lived for a time, communing with the Creator, until he had found his role.

Next, she spoke of the Great Flood. "That was the day the Water-Star broke! It was called Miloh. It fell down upon the earth and many people were drowned. Then God sent us another star, called Garbah, to suck up all the water and dry up the earth again!

There were very few survivors of this inundation. There was a man called Kanjipoh, who climbed up a high mountain and took with him many birds and animals. Everything that climbed up with him managed to survive. Kanjipoh had three sons namely Horo, Dogoh and Muran. Of these three sons, Dogoh became the ancestor of the Oromo people. Her prowess grew and one by one, a few adults joined in. This helped to increase her healing practice, since all now felt they could trust her.

One day, two young women arrived forcibly dragging between them a slightly older woman, who struggled against being restrained. She was their sister, they explained, and they did not know what to do with her. A fit had come over her a month before, and since then she had been out of her wits — completely mad! Hawecha looked into the woman's soul, and saw at once that the woman had been cursed. She could see who was behind this evil deed: a man who was jealous of the fact that she had produced three sons whereas his own wife was still barren after many years of marriage.

Dabassah had once asked her to help him perform the rituals. Having watched him attentively, surely she could remember somehow. Hawecha knew she could remove the curse.

She brought a stool outside from within her hut and asked the two young women to hold their older sister down upon it. Returning to her hut, she stoked up her fire. She needed one hundred and fourteen coffee beans. Counting hastily, she saw she had nowhere near enough! She scurried from hut to hut, begging the women to help her. At last, she had acquired the holy number. Quickly, she assembled all the paraphernalia she would need.

Recalling Dabassah's admonition to protect herself against evil, she found a large seed upon the ground and buried it beneath her tree, calling upon Sofmari to look after her. A change in the atmosphere told her he was with her in spirit. Now, she could not go wrong.

Hawecha heated the beans in cowfat in her mother's wooden coffee-bowl. She took out fifty-four beans, put them in a smaller wooden bowl and held this over the accursed woman's head. Using a wooden spoon, she flipped seven beans outwards to the east, west, south and north. Then, she laid seven of them upon the ground, widely spaced in a straight line.

Now she instructed the two women to help their sister walk upon each bean, beginning the walk with her right foot. Each bean had to be broken. There was a mighty struggle as they forced the woman's feet into position and made her stamp upon each bean. Hawecha knew the evil curse would break upon the seventh coffee bean. It was worth the struggle.

The woman was near to fainting by the time of the seventh satisfying "crack". Hawecha seeing that all desire to fight back had evaporated, allowed the woman to sit upon the ground between her two guardians whilst she prepared the next step.

This involved making seven small fires — a ritual which had originated from the Pleiades, the small cluster of stars not far from Sirius. It was a means of purification.

As Dabassah had done, she lit these fires some small distance apart; in a wavy line. The woman was helped to walk between them from one end to the other.

Taking a few twisted fibre threads, Hawecha knotted these together into one long rope, which she tied from one tree to another. The woman had to pass beneath this rope three times. When that was done, they helped her to walk away to the east, just a few steps, since by now the woman was scarcely able to move.

Now came the final healing. Hawecha buried the remaining coffee beans, brought a bowl of water from her hut and washed the woman's head with it. The woman attempted to stand up but instead fell into a dead faint. Hawecha and the two guardians heaved and panted as they laid her down upon Hawecha's bed. Gasping at their exertions, they too collapsed upon the ground; their harsh breath rasping within the small confines of the hut.

At last, Hawecha calmed down. It had been far more difficult than she had imagined. Yet, looking at her patient, she knew she had succeeded. The woman lay there placidly, with her hands gently folded across her breast. Behind her eyes lay an invisible smile. Yes, the curse had gone.

The woman awakened and the smile became reality. A look of love and gratitude shone in her eyes. They all sighed with relief. A few sips of water and the woman announced she was well enough to go home now.

She promised to give Hawecha a goat in payment. Hawecha doubted she would receive this munificent reward, but smiled graciously and bid them all a long life.

Two days later, a young boy came with the promised goat. It was the largest payment Hawecha had ever received. For a moment she was quite overcome. Then, having penned up her gift with her other goats, she disappeared inside her hut. There, with nobody to observe her, she broke into a wild and frenzied dance of jubilation. She danced until she dropped.

Only then did she remember to thank Sofmari.

# CHAPTER 40

There was no stopping Hawecha now. She had scaled the spiritual heights beyond any other woman that they knew of. Only the five high priests, the many ritual leaders and the Fathers of an eight-year cycle ranked above her. There were only three of those, one for each sacred site at which the *gadamoji* ceremonies were always held. She had truly joined the tribal hierarchy.

In recognition of her achievements, she was invited to participate in the next *gadamoji* ceremonies to be held at Tuqqa – the very place Hawecha as a small child had longed to go to. Its name had rung in her head like a loud cowbell. She set off with glee on her journey: not alone this time.

Quite a delegation embarked on the long trek southwards and then eastwards. Their leader was a high councillor, determined to attend one more ceremony. Looking at him, straight and proud upon his donkey, Hawecha had no qualms whatever as to his vigour. He might even live to see another *gadamoji* after this one.

She was not quite so certain that Qooyeh – his wife – would survive. She seemed frail. Frequent pauses were required so she could urinate behind a convenient bush or shrub. She grimaced with pain frequently, yet whenever Hawecha asked if she were well, Qooyeh admonished her. "You look after *you,* and I will look after *me!*" Hawecha left her alone.

Abdub had decided to join the party. It would be his first *gadamoji.* He was not particularly spiritual but he enjoyed 'a good crowd'. With him came a boisterous family.

Molu and Buleh, two brothers, had decided to accompany them for part of the way. They were moving southwards to join another clan and seek wives amongst them. Meanwhile, armed with spears, they would protect the group as it travelled.

Saqo had also decided to come, having, as he put it, nothing better to do with his life. His wife had died in childbirth and the baby had also died. Poor man. He needed something to occupy his mind other than feelings of guilt and endless recriminations.

He walked beside Hawecha, asking her endless questions. First about her herbal remedies and about Fugug and all the places she had seen. Later, the conversation turned a little more spiritual. She spoke of Suleh and the afterlife. She could see his wife holding their little son, throwing him up into the air and catching him again. One day, he would join them. Hawecha, sensing that she would die before he did, promised to help him find them. This comforted him greatly. It was a happier man who walked beside her now. The journey passed pleasantly and the days sped by. Indeed, Hawecha was scarcely aware of time.

At last the settlement lay before them, a little larger than the ceremonial village of her first *gadamoji* but otherwise identical. The only difference for Hawecha was that instead of being housed far to the left, she found herself given unprecedented honour.

She was domiciled in the hut of an official messenger. His wife allocated to Hawecha a bed to the rear of their home, patted her on the cheek and called her 'my adopted daughter'. Hawecha was delighted at this appellation and did her best to live up to it.

The next day she was called before the ritual leader. He bowed before her and bade her to sit beside him. He invited her in the name of all that the Oromo held holy to devote herself to improving the minds of the women present. He wished them to develop spiritually and had dreamed that she could do so. He had seen a star above her head, a bright and large one. Did she know which star it was?

Hawecha replied unhesitatingly. "Sirius. Sirius is my star-guide."

For the duration of the ceremonies, Hawecha did her best to comply with his request and insight. Her work kept her far removed from rituals at times to the extent that for her, it was hardly a ceremony. Her 'school' filled up with women and girls of all ages. They could not all attend at once — given their manifold duties. Hawecha was forced into endless repetitions. It was all she could do to bite her tongue and keep her irritation from flaring up.

One night, when her work for the day was long over, but the women were still singing outside, she fell into an uneasy sleep, a shallow one. She felt herself drifting off on a long silver cord floating above the earth. She could see a round rotating earth. The sun was a huge ball of fire around which it spun. The known world receded as she flew past it and into other worlds. Part of her lay terrified whilst the other part revelled in the journey. Of all the many adventures in her already unusual life, this was by the far the most enthralling. She clung to the silver cord and continued onwards.

She came to a great swirl of silver heat that thrust giant arms outwards in all directions from its epicentre. Somehow, she knew that she had just passed Sirius. In her dream-state, she sat up in astonishment.

Her dream did not terminate there, however. There was a sharp pull on her cord and she flew through the universe at even greater speed. At last she seemed to slow down. It felt as though somebody was guiding her towards her final destination. She saw hands pulling on her cord, slender-fingered, long and bony, perhaps twice the size of hers. More astonishingly, they were pale green and almost transparent.

Three figures stood before her. They were far taller than she was and thin. There was a shadowy quality to them as though they were not altogether real. She felt that if she poked her finger into one of them, it would meet no resistance. Looking upwards she saw their enormous eyes. Magnificent shining ovals stared down at her from a great height. Before she could express her fear, one of them spoke. The words emerged as if held together by a string: slowly and somewhat ponderously. She quite literally saw the words he uttered!

"We live here, Hawecha. We wanted you to see our world. You are so interested in the stars and planets and in the works of God that we thought you might like to see more. We are not like you, but we think and feel as you do."

Hawecha, nonplussed, stood and gaped at them.

A second figure spoke. "Please, do not be afraid of us. We are guides and teachers here. We mean you no harm."

Hawecha found her voice and as she spoke, her words seemed to float forth from her mouth in silence. "I know you are made by God because there is no dark grey in your auras."

The three figures spoke amongst themselves before the first one addressed her again.

"Please, ask us questions. We are here to teach you."

Hawecha floated about the ethers for a moment, thinking to herself. 'Where am I?'

"You have reached Druul, a planet in another world. We are very friendly towards those who dwell on Earth."

"Do you die?"

Her query surprised her, since she realized it was hardly polite. The figure beamed at her and replied that they did not. They had attained a world of peace where death did not occur. Only those who lived on earth had to face death.

"Must we all die? If you live forever, why can't we?"

The response was solemn. "You die until you live in peace with God and do not fight against the laws. Some people are sent back to earth time after time, until they learn this. It is the most important lesson there is, Hawecha. Some have been born a thousand times."

Hawecha shrank back somehow at these words. She managed to ask haltingly whether she had. The answer came ponderously.

"You have lived before Hawecha. You are near the end now. There may be a few faults on your conscience at the end of this life, but you will find your freedom soon enough."

"I feel somehow that you are right. I don't feel I am as pure as you are." Hawecha seemed to become a little smaller.

"Ask Sofmari to help you. He is as pure as we are. And he has had many lives."

The vision faded and she was swept through a darkening tunnel until — quite abruptly — she found herself sitting up in bed.

There was no more sleep for Hawecha that night. The three teachers had given her knowledge of such magnitude that she needed time to reflect upon it — before daybreak came with all its mundane matters.

She wondered if other worlds were inhabited and understood at once that they were. She wondered where the silver cord had originated and found that it had emerged from her own breast. She wondered what she had done in other lifetimes and saw herself as a small brown girl running to her mother's arms. "No, that is this lifetime. That is my own mother." She tried to cast her mind further back in time; all she saw was herself flying up through a dark tunnel and being welcomed by spirits whose great golden wings enfolded her gently. They carried her aloft to a small green hill. "So there are other forms of life too," she thought, realising she had somehow recalled a previous death.

The experience was too much for her; she felt unable to continue further. Numbed and shaken, she stumbled through the warren of huts towards the exit.

As usual, she sought solace beneath the heavens. There was Sirius almost directly overhead. All was well, then. As long as she could find her star-guide, she would manage life somehow. As for the distant past, she felt it best forgotten. She would work hard on making this life the one that pleased God most.

Recalling the words of her teacher, she called upon Sofmari. Perhaps he could relieve her anxiety. She heard a low and gentle voice.

"Dear one, I am known as the Man-With-a-Thousand-Faces. I do not care how many faces I have had. Some were old and some were young. Some were of other tribes. Some were of people not on earth any more: ancient, ancient souls. I like to teach. I assume whichever face I feel will teach best. See my face now, Hawecha, and know me!"

She peered out into the darkness. He was not there. She closed her eyes and looked inwards. A glow filled her inner mind and gradually a man emerged. He was quite tall and wore violet robes that shimmered. His demeanour was serene. His eyes were of an amazing blue. Hawecha recoiled. In her world, all eyes were brown.

"You are not Oromo!" she shouted, then bit her tongue in remorse. His reply was kind. "My eyes are made by God. I awakened one morning with them. The eyes are the true soul speaking. Study my eyes, Hawecha, and tell me what you see."

Hawecha looked fearfully and then with greater boldness. "Kind and wise. Friendly to me. Helpful, wonderful." He smiled and said he had to leave her. "The sun will rise soon, Hawecha. Speak of what you have seen. It may help a few of the others."

She found herself alone.

Turning to the east, she saw a thin line of pale gold above the horizon. "I must run to the river and wash myself well. I am not ready for people yet."

The water was cold. Hawecha discarded her goatskins and plunged in. She wanted some sort of shock to pull her back. She had promised to teach six women today how to sew and clean babies. As the waters covered her shoulders, she wondered how she would face them. And to whom could she speak to about Druul and the three teachers? Who would believe she had seen Sofmari?

As she emerged and donned her goatskins, she decided to teach only what she had promised. The rest would have to wait. It was like a secret and she was afraid to share it.

On her way back towards the settlement, a reddish stone caught her eye. She stooped and picked it up. "Teach when you are ready. Some will want to listen." She thanked the stone for sharing with her its spiritual essence, tied it up in a corner of her goatskin, and continued on her way.

# CHAPTER 41

Her chance came one day as she was teaching some of the women a new prayer. One of them emerged from her concentrated efforts to announce that she had seen a star and that it seemed somebody was waving to them from there. Hawecha decided to make the most of this opening.

Before long, a discussion had arisen with contributions from several sources. One had dreamed of a small blue star. Another had heard a voice calling her as she slept: a voice she did not recognize. It said it came from the Pleiades.

Hawecha found the path made smooth. She spoke of the three teachers she had met, of their kindness to her and – hesitantly – of their enormous luminous eyes. "Not round like ours, but long – like a date." None had seen such, but since the information came from Hawecha, all believed her.

She spoke of Sofmari and his violet clothing. Two old women confirmed that their husbands had seen him in dreams.

The morning passed pleasantly and Hawecha felt at peace. It seemed that esoteric matters were quite acceptable if the subject were carefully broached.

That night, she dreamed of a single being; short and of whitish skin, with eyes somewhat smaller than those of her three teachers. The being explained melifluously that it lived on the small, heavy, invisible star that revolved around Sirius.

Hawecha had heard of this star from Dabassah. According to him, it only passed their way once every fifty years. Hawecha asked what the inhabitants did on 'the other days' and felt a gentle smile upon her as the being replied. "We work all year round. Our sense of time is different from yours, but your learned astronomers have understood our cycle.

When we can see you, we know it is time for one of us to teach. We just wait to find out who will be the pupil."

She understood that this time *she* was the one and waited for her lesson. "You have to ask, you know," her new friend announced. "I do not know what interests you."

The conversation revealed that her teacher — although sexless — had choosen to be 'more male than female': she could therefore properly address the speaker as a he.

Having sorted out this necessary etiquette, Hawecha learned that he could count, could see colours and could see Hawecha's aura. His own was sometimes red and sometimes a deep, deep blue.

Further questioning on her part elicited the information that there were thousands of inhabitants on his world and that every single one of them was a teacher. They took turns, not caring how long they waited. His parting advice to her was to study life on other stars and planets. Most had some sort of life upon them. Hawecha, thinking of the countless pinpoints of light overhead felt somewhat daunted at this prospect but assured him she would make every effort — when time permitted.

The next day, it transpired that a young woman whom Hawecha had uncharitably defined as stupid, had also spoken to a being from another place. This being came from Venus. He was immensely tall and seemed to vibrate as he spoke. She had asked how old he was and had learned that he did not know: he lived eternally and age was therefore meaningless to him.

Hawecha wondered if any female would present herself. Two nights later she dreamed of an almost invisible, shadowy form who announced it was female and had come in answer to her question. The magnitude of this celestial collaboration astounded her. Did they all know of her most intimate thoughts? She was told that they knew those on earth who were willing to teach other people. From childhood, they had known of her fascination with the stars. Who better than she — a promising teacher of good repute? Flattered, Hawecha plied this 'female' with questions.

She learned that this teacher lived on one of the stars used in the Oromo calendar. "I am old, Hawecha, far older than anybody living in *your* world. I am waiting to welcome any of you who wish to come here.

Your world is full of people whose lives began on the stars, long, long ago. Some of them want to visit one day. So, I wait."

This news made Hawecha's head spin. She at once crept out into the night and searched the heavens above. Dabassah had told her that Suleh now lived on Venus. Had she come from there originally? Venus was not visible. Hawecha decided to call Suleh and ask her. It transpired that Suleh had been born on Earth but enjoyed visiting other worlds. After sojourns on Sirius and the Pleiades, she had decided to settle on Venus where she would dwell for many aeons.

Hitherto, it had never occurred to Hawecha to wonder whether the guides and teachers had homes. Now she felt relieved to find they had. This fact made them somehow more 'human' and more accessible.

"You will need many lifetimes to locate us all, Hawecha." Suleh laughed as the vision of her faded.

In the morning as Hawecha crossed the compound, she suddenly realised she was walking through a pale blue shimmering line, like the ones she had seen from Mount Abunu. She paused and crossed it again. A *gadamoji* who had been observing her spoke up quite suddenly. "Yes, I saw it too." She whirled around in surprise.

"Did you know it had a numerical value?" the old man asked. Hawecha shook her head. He sat her down beside him on a wooden stool and explained that every such line had a number. You had to close your eyes to learn it. His father had taught him this many years before. Hawecha closed her eyes and the number sixty-two popped into her head. She asked the old man what it meant and he instructed her to close her eyes again.

"It means rapid spiritual growth," she learned. "Good, at this rate, I shall soon become a high priest." Dismayed at her audacity, Hawecha clapped a hand over her mouth and gasped. "I have gone too far now. Hard, hard labour will rid me of my disgusting arrogance!" Making her excuses to the old man, she departed in search of work.

# CHAPTER 42

By the time of the ceremony for the first-born, Hawecha was utterly worn out. She had taught (and she had also learned) in a seemingly never-ending cycle. When it came time for the final feast she had sunk into a deep slumber — right there upon her stool. The women took pity on her and carried her to her bed. She knew nothing of this until daybreak came with a great clamouring.

She yawned and stretched mightily, staggered through the doorway to perform somewhat sketchy ablutions and thanked all the women who had cared for her. It was time to go home.

Hawecha found preparations for their departure well under way. Qooyeh, who despite Hawecha's misgivings had survived the rigours of the journey, scolded her for her tardiness. Hawecha apologised ruefully and hastened to load up her donkey. At last, they were ready.

The men-folk had decided they would detour through Tuqqa itself, since they seldom had a chance to see a thriving trading centre.

Two hours later, they came upon a great hurly-burly. Trade goods were piled up on the ground here and there with vendors and purchasers gesticulating wildly over them. Goats were clustered to one side, with heavy bartering in progress. A small flock of sheep was fought over by three determined young men. Four horses stamped their feet and snorted in their war against the flies. Clay pots, gourds and leather containers of all sizes occupied a space beneath a large and shady tree. Metal bangles clanked: iron shoulder-ornaments glinted in the sun.

Men, women and children filled the skies with voices of every kind, some hoarse, many vociferous, a few elated, many disheartened.

Hawecha walked around from stall to stall, from heap to heap, from argument to argument. It was her delight to observe and listen. Only once was she tempted to buy a thin, twisted iron bracelet. She eyed this wistfully and then resisted. With her seemingly endless peregrinations about the earth, the fewer items she possessed the better. No, not one bangle did she truly want.

The traders were Somalis, haughty men, who hawked and spat frequently, as if to show their disdain of the Oromo 'lesser mortals' who had come to view their wares. Some wore long white robes and others long shirts over baggy trousers. Many wore turbans, some with a long loose flap hanging down to one side of their head. All the men were bearded: some were vigorous and dark, whilst others showed threads of grey. One or two were 'hennaed.' Hawecha found this use of orange dye unbecoming to an elder — as if a little colour would bring back his youth!

Only two women were visible, unkempt and wearing filthy garments, shocking examples of their sex. Yet it was these two who oversaw the spice market. The Oromo women held their breath and averted their gazes as they made a few purchases.

Tethered behind the market-place were many camels. Having brought this merchandise upon their backs from some point far to the north, they now rested briefly from their labours.

Each trader had by now amassed a goodly quantity of cowries. Some brought out large silver coins from hidden pockets to exchange for goats. These coins were known as 'Mariam Teresas' after the Austrian queen whose likeness they bore. Hawecha asked to see one, finding it astounding that the coin should have travelled so far. She held it in her palm, studying the ruler's visage.

"What a haughty woman. She eats too much. And what an ugly nose," Hawecha mused. She turned the coin over and wondered what sort of bird it was that had two heads. 'Ostira' must be a peculiar land, with its odd-looking women and its even odder birds. She returned the coin scornfully, jutting out her lip.

As soon as the camels had drunk their fill from the nearby well, the traders would once more set off in search of goods to barter. One of the caravans would be heading northwards passing near Hawecha's village. Abdub had spoken to the leader and they were invited to travel in his company — provided they did not slow him down. What a novelty for them. The following morning, they set off at a brisk pace determined to keep up with the long-legged camels.

In the course of their journey, much information was exchanged.

Hawecha learned of new tribes that lived to the south — new to her, that is. Ahmed told her of the Loikop who were at war with their cousins, the Maasai. "Both have fathered fierce warriors and both sides are well armed with weapons made by their blacksmiths. They have fought each other now for many, many years — even though they speak the same language or dialects thereof. I don't know who will win this time." He explained that their neighbours, the Rendille, had withdrawn into their desert fastness until it was all over.

He spoke of Mount Marsabetti which lay in Borana hands. The Borana were an Oromo offshoot who had migrated further south. "Once, the mountain belonged to the Loikop, you know. Your people stole it from them." Hawecha had heard of this holy mountain and was shocked to discover that it was not God who had given it her cousins. Ahmed laughed at her naivety and cock-eyed view of history. "We men know better. Your God may have given you this or that originally, but now the world is in the hands of men. It is *we* who decide our destiny."

He spoke disparagingly of his God, Allah. "We pray, we pray, we pray. Then we fast, and we pray again," he complained. "Nothing happens. I must still put shoes upon my feet and food into my children's mouths. I must still impregnate my wife each year to make sure I am taken care of in my old age. I tell you nothing changes. It is all a waste of time."

"Perhaps you have not lived long enough to see the results of your prayers," Hawecha remarked tartly. "Mine are answered frequently, sometimes within the same day."

It seemed Ahmed disliked the turn the conversation was taking. Their philosophical discussion ended rather abruptly when he declared he had to move on now, 'night and day,' until he reached Aksum.

With much yelling and bellowing — and no farewell — his caravan marched off.

# CHAPTER 43

The journey home was uneventful and so were the ensuing months. Hawecha found herself as busy as ever, dealing with an expanded healing practice as well as with regular teachings.

To the north of Oromia, events took on a deeply disturbing note. Tales of war came their way. The battles and bloodshed seemed to increase in scope.

One day, a Gabbra caravan passed through, on its return journey south to their homeland. There were in fact three caravans which had combined forces to travel together: such was the prevailing danger. They carried no merchandise, for all had been sold — or stolen by armed bandits. The north was in a state of complete unpheaval, it was said.

Of the three leaders, one was an old man with a fine beard whilst the other two were his nephews. It was too dangerous to take their womenfolk with them since it was not worth risking their being raped. Wives and sisters had therefore been left at home. Small wonder the men were dour and subdued.

Hawecha reviewed what she knew of 'foreign' history. She recalled that — in long years past — the northern states had come under the Emperor Fasil. He had been the first to create a fixed place of residence, selecting Gonder as his seat of power. There, he had built himself a great multi-storeyed castle. Hawecha had heard of this 'mountain of stone' which resembled three huge villages built one on top of another.

As for more recent times, Hawecha remembered that Ras Sihul Mikael, who had ruled Tigre Province during her youth, had strangled the Emperor Ioas approximately ten years earlier. Sihul Mikael had been *de facto* ruler of Ethiopia for forty years, all told. He had finally been defeated, just two years ago.

Nowadays, she had heard there was no federal rulership. Princes came to power and lost that power in rapid succession. One region fought another. The peasantry suffered great hardships from the ravages of these incessant civil wars. She asked the traders for an accurate assessment of the situation. The old man shook his head sorrowfully and showed the villagers his musket; the first Hawecha had seen. He explained that there were many thousands of these guns about now and that each prince had his own army, equipped with the deadly weapon.

He fired at a crow to show how it worked. Hearing the great 'bang!' of a gunshot and seeing the crow dead upon the ground, Hawecha's heart almost stopped. An icy fear crept into her veins. How could a simple spear stand up against such a weapon as this? In her vivid imagination, Liban fell dead at her feet!

As they sat around a great fire that night, sharing food and information, Hawecha's thoughts turned to yet another danger that faced them all. She asked them if they ever dealt in slaves, a nefarious trade, begun long, long ago.

To her relief, they all swore that they did not, for to sell a fellow human was against the laws of nature. They themselves — like the Christians — preferred a more modest means of earning a living: one that might be considered noble. Certainly, they made a profit but they also provided invaluable services, keeping the people of the far south stocked up on necessities, as well as bringing them up to date on modern inventions and new imports. That was, after all, the point of engaging in foreign trade.

They emphasised that the slave trade was a particularly Muslim vice. Those traders became exceedingly wealthy selling their commodity to Arabia — just like livestock. One of the nephews described the human market-place and the auctions that were held. He had seen these at Diredawa, a great inland trading centre in the north. The state of these poor humans was indescribable; he deplored their state of mental suffering as well as their physical degradation.

Hawecha fell into a silent prayer. With all these threats surrounding them, would the Oromo survive? She turned to the old man and asked him what he thought.

"Your people have been here for a very long time now, Hawecha. You were the very first people here. I have seen your circles of standing stones to the south of us. I pass them every year and marvel at them. I understand from your experts that they represent the Oromo calendar.

Our forefathers spoke of those monoliths."

He seemed lost in thought for a time, then nodded his head vigorously. He turned to Hawecha. "Yes, your people were here first." He paused and grinned, becoming suddenly handsome as he did so. "And with your God to look after you, I suspect you will also be the last." His kind remark helped to relieve the tension and they broke into laughter.

It was by now the middle of the night. One by one, the villagers stumbled off to bed. Only Hawecha and a handful of the men-folk remained to talk beside the fire. Hawecha poked it and added a great branch, to keep them all warm as conversation was resumed.

Saqo brought up another subject, that of the ivory trade. He had heard it was a lucrative line of business. The traders admitted they were all involved in it. They described how the great elephant tusks were loaded onto camels and then transported to Massawa for shipment to far-off lands. The younger nephew spoke of a human caravan he had seen, carrying these weighty objects on foot with several to share one tusk.

Hawecha shook her head in sadness. It seemed the human lot was not always a happy one. How fortunate she was to belong to an enlightened people.

It was not often that Hawecha had an opportunity to quiz outsiders on the greater world beyond Liban. She was anxious to make the most of the traders' sojourn, yet she wished now to turn her thoughts away from woe.

Searching for a cheerful topic, Hawecha asked if they had heard of the Falasha people, who had a different religion and claimed to have come from somewhere much further north.

Much to Hawecha's amazement, the uncle broke into vociferous complaint. He described them as perverted and preoccupied with sex. It seemed the women made small figurines out of clay. By far, the most popular consisted of a man and woman together in bed hugging each other and who knew what else. He professed himself profoundly shocked at such profanities being sold on the open market. Sex was surely meant to be a private matter. They all nodded in agreement.

At last they left, promising to pass this way again on the next southbound journey. In addition to their much-needed salt, which was mined in the land of the Afars, they would bring them new commodities.

These he enumerated on his fingers. He would bring them brass wire and brass pots that never broke. He would bring cotton clothing. He would select colourful glass beads that came from a place called Venice. Finally, for the women, he would bring *kohl,* with which to blacken their eyelids as Muslim women did.

Hawecha laughed. She could not imagine herself putting black rings around her eyes; let other women do so, if they liked. Nor could she see herself wearing cotton clothes. Perhaps she was singularly old-fashioned, but goatskins were what suited her best.

As the camels disappeared over the horizon, Hawecha found herself feeling frightened again. She was plagued by troublesome thoughts of war, rape, slaves and guns. She could not shake off this mood of strange disquiet, no matter how hard she worked.

Each evening, she walked across the plains and even around in large circles, hoping to tire herself out. The thoughts persisted. Then *one* thought. Guns!

# CHAPTER 44

The mood persisted for several days before poor Hawecha, whose life had been so troubled by terrifying dreams, once more found herself in the midst of one.

First, she saw a fierce male lion with long, shaggy mane roaming about within their compound. It was eating bags of grain. Hawecha wondered what kind of lion ate millet especially when there were goats about?

Next, three stars fell on her head, shouting "Woe, woe is me!" in unison.

Following this image, she had seen two groups of men in white fighting each other. Seven muskets now lay upon the ground before her, pointing to the north.

Lastly, she saw a vast expanse of blood on the ground. The air was filled with loud shrieking. The world was full of war. Then Sirius told her that in order to avoid the war, she must take the people elsewhere, out of the direct path of battle. She herself could see that safety lay to the south. She saw a green land there, where blessed silence reigned.

In the morning, a harried Hawecha sent three young boys out to ask the men-folk to gather together beneath her tree. It took some time before they all arrived.

Calmly, she described her dream, clear that it foretold a war of great proportions. Men armed with guns would come against them soon. She wanted protection along the route to the south, in case of an attack from the rear. They must prepare.They had only six weeks in which to do so. She asked them to send out messengers to all the surrounding villages and encourage them to join the plan for withdrawal.

All the smiths set to work at their smithies, smelting and hammering, mending weapons, working the bellows and hammering yet again. Soon, two hundred arrows had been fashioned from the raw iron ore. A week later, forty spears had been added to the arsenal. The warriors were out of practice. In their village Saqo took charge. They practised hand-to-hand combat, feinting and wrestling, doing elaborate footwork and aiming at hastily-rigged targets. They worked at honing their skills and sharpening their senses until it was too dark to continue.

Tales of heroes and prowess were told and retold to the young boys all of whom were armed with sharp knives, as well as the smaller bows they could all handle.

Some would die in battle, but if the enemy attacked as they travelled, then so would a few of them. This was as it should be. The Oromo would never fight amongst themselves but to kill an outside enemy was an act of glory — to be immortalized if they reached the age of *gadamoji* when they boasted of their exploits.

At last, the men-folk were ready. Thirty or forty families from outlying settlements gathered outside the gates in the ensuing days. Hawecha ran from one head of household to the next asking them all for patience. She sensed that more were on the way to join them and so it proved to be. One day, she knew the last family had arrived. Now they numbered three or four hundred people.

For the last time, Hawecha sat beneath her tree with her back to the east and to her childhood. Above her head, the breeze created a gentle susurration among the leaves.

With Hawecha now acknowledged as their leader, they turned southwards fleeing from impending doom. Driving vast herds and flocks before them, as well as a few camels, they made slow progress. Hawecha felt like a great queen, leading her people to what she earnestly hoped would be lasting peace and prosperity.

Saqo, who proved to be a brilliant military strategist, had organised their warriors. Twenty or so led the way. At the rear of their column came another forty whilst the remainder flanked them, left and right. Hawecha felt well-protected.

After three weeks of journeying, news caught up with them in the form of a small band of sorry-looking refugees.

Ras Asrat of Gojam had made war on the ruler of Welega. His vast army had swept down from the north, pressing the enemy further and further southwards, until they had penetrated Oromo lands. The Ras's army had cut a wide swathe through Oromo territory.

Brave Oromo warriors — caught in between two foreign armies who were at each other's throats — had resisted fiercely. As Hawecha had foreseen, muskets and rifles had triumphed. The news was shattering: it was said that untold hundreds of Oromo had perished. Those who survived were now retreating southwards.

One old woman sobbed that she had seen her two daughters raped and then stabbed repeatedly until death mercifully ended their shame and pain. Another had seen two of her sons shot dead. A third had seen a soldier grab her little girl by the arm and hack her to pieces in mid-air. A young man had had one leg chopped off and now hobbled beside them on makeshift crutches, blood still seeping from his stump.

The tales of atrocity piled up until Hawecha felt she could bear no more. Once again her people had been mowed down and diminished. Like children plucking off the petals of a flower one by one, so had many Oromo petals fallen. It seemed they were at the mercy of devastatingly powerful external forces: pestilence, famine and war. None were of their own making. For the second time in her life, Hawecha wondered if they would recover.

They gathered around the fire that night to pray for the souls of the dead, promising to join them in the hereafter and give them solace for their pain. Meanwhile, they begged their ancestors to comfort the new arrivals and help them build new shelters.

After three weeks of journeying, they reached a place where Sirius advised them to settle. It was not as green as Hawecha had expected but the soil was rich enough, the trees tall enough and the grass sufficiently plentiful for them to contemplate a new beginning.

Once more, from next to nothing, new huts were constructed: new logs dragged into new huts to separate new sleeping areas from new sitting areas. Again, livestock was carefully penned. The work was hard and tedious, yet in time the land proved fertile. Their millet flourished and they celebrated the harvest according to tradition, with songs and special prayers.

They formed a large colony here to the south where it seemed no human had preceded them. Marriages were arranged between the clans. Imperceptibly, the community began to flourish.

# CHAPTER 45

Hawecha felt old now: old before her time. Age had crept up on her without her being aware of it. She noticed that small girls were now married women and first-born sons had grown quite suddenly into warriors. Her own age-mates were beginning to evince infirmities and chronic illnesses. A few had already died.

Now, when she looked at her reflection in the river or in a rain puddle, she saw that deep furrows ran down her cheeks and creased her forehead horizontally. Her eyes seemed to have a perpetually threatened look about them. Her whole face spoke of endless worrying and fretting. She was remarkably fit and energetic for her age, yet of late she had been assailed by pains in her lower back and cramping in her left side.

Talking to Suleh, Sofmari or Sirius was of no comfort to her. She realised that, for her, life was nearly over. Her dreams supported her in this knowledge, for she often saw her mother's face: not speaking, just there. She felt closer to God too and understood that she had climbed a high metaphysical mountain to get there.

"You are old, Hawecha," she said to herself. "You have seen too much of life; more than sixty years of it. What are you going to do about it?"

She sat down on a small hill overlooking her village thinking of how much trust they all placed in her. "Too much!" she thought. "When I die, there will be nobody to prophecy for them and protect them from disasters." She wept for her poor people.

Then she recalled that they had had leaders before her — both male and female. She was but one of them. There were several spiritual lineages. Surely, other leaders would follow. She remembered her development step by step from frightened and humble origins. Up and up she had climbed.

Quite suddenly, she grinned. Life was not quite over yet. There was perhaps time for one last and glorious adventure.

Another *gadamoji* ceremony was to take place shortly. As usual, participants would soon make their way to one of the traditional sites. Should she go to Tuqqa again or perhaps somewhere new? She had heard there would be a large group gathering at Negeleh. Far, far away! Good, then she would have a long adventure.

She felt drawn to visit Mega. Well, she could go there too. She would pass by there first. It would be a long detour but she felt herself undaunted. "I want to spend time with one high priest before I die. Let it be the one who dwells at Mega!" Should she also go to Gaayo, the scene of the lawmakers' gathering? No, there were too many painful memories.

In her mind, she began to plan the journey; a slow sweep further south followed by a long trek facing due west. She would spend a few days in Mega, hopefully with the high priest, before continuing further. From Mega, she would have to turn north-east. She would have to ask for directions to Negeleh. With so many travellers on the roads, that should present no problem. How long would it take her? One month, she supposed. With much to occupy her now, she began her preparations.

She announced to the community that she would discontinue her work as a healer.

"I will die quite soon and until then I need more time for myself. You must learn to live without me and you must start this very minute. I have to prepare myself in my own way."

As if to emphasise her point, she scattered upon the ground her remaining remedies: twigs, leaves and powders. Then she stamped firmly down upon them. "Now, that is the end. All of you have seen it!"

There was nothing more to be said. Her old donkey had died by now and so had its son. It was her third beast of burden that carried her precious belongings. As she loaded it up, talking to it to keep it calm, she mused upon her material status. They all assumed she must be rich by now. Rumours had it that she possessed valuable horses, vast herds of goats, many excess bags of salt, a stack of salt-bars and even piles of the silver 'Mariam Teresas' coins. They said she was the richest woman in all the land.

Hawecha shook with silent laughter. If the gossips could only see her now! All she owned in the world were fifteen goats, which she would distribute among these villagers. One hut, which she would offer to the village as an extra guest house, one shoulder-ornament, which she would pass on to an expectant mother, one cracked wooden cup, which she would take with her for the many coffee rituals she hoped to attend, two small wooden bowls, which would also go with her, three surplus goatskins and her sleeping skins. One bar of salt, a pinch of cumin; two leather straps, three fibre ropes and one donkey. Mentally, she added two panniers.

Not her mother's ceremonial coffee-bowl: that had cracked in to two six months before. Hawecha laughed out loud. Why, she was probably poorer than they were!

Having made her parting gifts she set off boldly without glancing back.

# CHAPTER 46

Hawecha pushed onwards. Already, she had been 'on the road' for more than a week, following goat tracks and well-worn cattle paths, picking her way over open grassland or through clumps of trees and bushes. Countless other footprints marked her progress; not all human or of domestic livestock. Once, a lion had padded along this way: once, a snake had wound and slithered across her path with a curious sideways motion. There were many birds 'walking' beside her — some clearly in a great hurry, whilst others had adopted a more stately pace.

When she tired of gazing down at her feet, there were many interesting cloud formations to amuse her and guide her; as they often did. "Not so fast, Hawecha: you will tire yourself out!" said a great wisp of high white feathering.

A single puffball later warned her to rest beneath the nearest tree. Late one afternoon, three small clouds told her to search for a suitable campsite before she got too tired.

Sometimes they referred to lofty matters. Great towering banks spoke to her of the Oromo of the future: "They will be educated, but in different ways. They will spread much further south in time." As she pondered upon these one-day changes, another small puffball — as if reading her mind — added: "yes, there will still be *gadamoji* ceremonies!"

She met people along the way, all of whom were pleased to accompany her for some small distance. Many offered her shelter for the night and she was usually glad to accept. At last, she turned to face due west.

Once in a while, the cramp in her left side slowed her down. There were always settlements where she could rest. As her journey lengthened, she seemed to require more and more pauses. Had she been foolish to embark on this crazy venture? No! her heart sang out. But it had to be the last.

She was never alone, for many were heading towards Mega. Large herds of goats were being driven to the weekly market: a few Gabbra camels heavily laden with grass mats passed her by. Donkeys laden with all manner of personal belongings trotted along, sometimes goaded by the flick of a light switch, or a heavier rhino-hide whip.

An elderly man of noble mien rode beside her for two whole days. He was an expert on time and on the Oromo calendar. He would be one of the advisors for the *gadamoji* ceremony.

Since the elders were only just now entering their 'sacred time' when they purified themselves for the coming rituals, another month remained before the ceremony would begin. They ambled along at a gentle pace, unhurried and untroubled.

Mega was a-throb with market day, yet Hawecha marched right through the trading centre without pause. She was too old to barter and haggle. She had felt a subtle change come over her; perhaps like the *gadamoji,* she too was leaving behind the profane. The time-expert applauded her strength of character. Hawecha, desiring to return the compliment suggested that she read his aura if he agreed, of course. He bowed his head and asked her to be scrupulously honest. He too was entering the sacred time.

"You are wise, careful with words and honest. You are much liked and people listen to you."

He bowed again, drinking in her words of praise. Hawecha resumed on a sadder note.

"You have a wife who is quite ill — too ill to accompany you now."

Startled, the elder gasped at her perspicacity and asked her how she knew this.

"I see it somehow. They say I have a strange ability to see what others do not see. It is not with my outer eyes that I see these matters. It comes from somewhere inside." Her companion nodded. "It is as they say. You have been chosen by God. It is from there that your special power comes."

As they rode along the now more populous pathway, Hawecha asked him about his own profession. She had understood very little of what Dabassah had tried to instil in her of their stars and the complex workings of their calendar. She knew there were twenty-seven stars which governed their daily lives and that some were more significant than others. She knew that Sirius was deemed the most important one of all to those who pursued a spiritual path. Beyond these bare bones, she professed herself profoundly ignorant. Would he, with all his vast knowledge, enlighten her?

The time-expert was delighted. He had had no pupil for seven years now and his own son had died three years before. There was nobody to inherit his knowledge from him. If he passed some of it on to this woman well, perhaps she would in turn pass it on to others. He embarked on a long and complex discourse. From it, Hawecha drew forth a few salient points.

There were twelve stars which took it in turn to help all teachers. Five stars were visible, the rest were not. Seven of the twelve told each teacher what he needed to know, or *she,* he hastened to add. Each of these twelve stars controlled the world for a period of eight years, namely the length of one entire age-set.

As he spoke, he reeled off names which fell melifluously from his tongue — like drops of cooling water. Darar, Fulas, Libas, Mogis . . . Mardit . . . Zara. It was as if he spoke a holy language, entirely different to the Oromifta of daily life. How she loved this man. Not as a woman loves a lover, but for his gift of knowledge. Hawecha felt that God had brought them together to make the journey smoother for them both.

He continued with an explanation of people's names, and how these too were controlled by the stars. By combining star lore with numerology, one could analyse a person's character. It all depended on your name.

The seven invisible stars had the power to name a person. They sent their power to Sirius, which in turn sent it down to you; therefore, every single person was named by one of the seven stars. Through mathematical calculations, it was possible to know which star had named who.

Hawecha got lost in the complex lesson. She almost wished she hadn't asked him for his knowledge. Yet she kept her questions courteous and tried to appreciate his responses. His wisdom had been acquired from a conscientious father. How glad she was that *her* knowledge depended mainly on quick flashes of insight.

She nodded sleepily upon her donkey, as he began to explain the fine nuances of their calendar, naming the stars one by one. *Garba Duraa, Garba Dullacha, Bita Qaraa ... Lumaasa . . . Algaajima.* The names rolled over her weary head. On the point of slipping sideways in a doze, she abruptly came back to full consciousness, awakened by her sixth sense. The settlement lay just ahead.

Hawecha explained that she wished to ask if the high priest would see her. They stopped at the entrance and asked an old woman if he had arrived yet. "We expect him tomorrow, child." Hawecha was much amused. Many years had passed since anybody had addressed her in this manner. Age was relative, then and perhaps she looked younger than she felt.

"Mother, please tell him that Hawecha wishes to speak with him before the ceremonies begin. I have need of his advice." She pointed to two trees beneath which she would sleep. They agreed that a messenger would be sent to fetch her.

Hawecha realised she was not meant to be gregarious or garrulous. Two days of incessant conversation had worn her out.

Sighing with relief at her new-found solitude, she watered her donkey, gobbled a few lumps of chewy goat meat, made up her pile of skins beneath the trees and sank down to rest.

# CHAPTER 47

"Are you Hawecha?" Two days had elapsed and a young boy stood before her. Hawecha grinned ruefully at herself: she had expected a more illustrious messenger. "Pride, Hawecha," she thought. "Your pride will surely be your downfall."

She had asked if she could meet the high priest outside the ceremonial settlement in order for them both to enjoy a little privacy. It seemed he had concurred. She was brought to him in a shady spot, not far off.

He sat upon his stool awaiting her arrival. As she approached she felt the strength of his aura. Aware that there were only five high priests of the entire tribe and that before her sat one of the two most important of those five, Hawecha was suddenly tongue-tied. She stood as tradition demanded, unable to address him properly.

He on his part beheld a tired and travel-worn woman of advancing years, whose fame had reached far and wide. He too was nonplussed: was she in some way not his equal? He found his voice at last and invited Hawecha to sit down. He asked her how he could assist her. "You are close to God now, Hawecha. You receive all your news from the Great Creator. What can I, a poor mortal, have to offer you?"

Hawecha wanted somebody to judge her before she died. She needed to know if he could read her aura. He was the son of the high priest who had spoken up for her all those years before. Surely, he also could see what others could not see?

The sage did not disappoint her. He half-closed his eyes and proceeded to speak in a soft, remote voice.

"You work hard and are very disciplined. You get what you want from people; you somehow manage to convince them." He paused as he studied her more deeply. "You have an inquisitive nature and are mature in your thinking. You have much knowledge by now." Then he shook his head from side to side.

"You are proud at times, Hawecha. That is your only sin. You think you are above the people somehow. You are not! Beware of your haughtiness."

He opened his eyes and gazed at her. Hawecha bowed her head in shame. Was he not absolutely correct in his assessment of her? Had she not condemned this self-same unsaintly trait in herself? The remainder of her life would have to be spent in some kind of penance. She wished most sincerely to improve and in a moment of inspiration asked him what he suggested.

She was astonished at his reply. "Go back to work, Hawecha, for your time has not yet come. You still have several years of life left to you. Use them wisely. Work until you die ... do not sit and wait for death to come."

He shifted about on his stool. "I think you should resume your healing or teaching or both if you have the stamina to do so."

There was nothing more to be said. Hawecha thanked him for his kindness and promised to obey him. Returning to where she had left her donkey, she strapped on her panniers and loaded her few possessions.

She had been told that a well-marked track led to Negeleh. She headed in that direction.

# CHAPTER 48

It was a long way to Negeleh and Hawecha was often faint from weariness. She had much to think of and sometimes forgot to eat at the proper time. It was a difficult decision: to teach or to resume healing? She knew she did not have sufficient strength for both. She turned the two options round and round in her mind, asking for omens to help her reach the right answer.

In the end, a small white feather lying on the path in front of her gave her what she needed. "It is better to teach, Hawecha." She neared Negeleh feeling much relieved.

She realised she was now traversing Fugug, the land of the Ancestors. Hawecha remembered that 'something bad had happened' and still she did not know what. Perhaps a disease had caused them to disperse or possibly an ancient war?

Hawecha hated not knowing. Alas, there was no Dabassah about now to answer any of her questions. Nor had he answered them then, as she recalled. So, the truth would never be known. She abandoned this frustrating line of thought and focused on the path instead. It was broad now, with many donkey hoof-marks etched upon it. She could almost hear them braying.

A group of girls were walking along the path: some carried clay pots of water on their heads, whilst a few also carried the more old-fashioned giraffe-neck water containers. Hawecha addressed the eldest and asked how far it was to the settlement. Only an hour or two longer, it transpired. The girl boldly asked her who she was and why she travelled alone. "I am Hawecha. I am always alone, child."

The girl whispered to a couple of the younger ones and sent them off to the village to advise the women of Hawecha's imminent arrival. Together, the remainder accompanied Hawecha, discussing the impending ceremonies. There were twenty-four elders to become *gadamoji* this year.

Hawecha was pleased. She needed a large crowd around her once more.

As they neared the gate, Hawecha was astonished to see a crowd of women waiting for her. As she approached, they broke into a great and loud ululation of welcome. Hawecha was utterly overwhelmed and fought to hold back tears of emotion.

She was escorted to the hut of one of the high councillors and made to feel at home there. She sank down with relief upon the bed provided, asked for a little water and then fell into a long doze.

Much refreshed, Hawecha walked around the compound asking which experts were present this time. To her joy, there were several. She was introduced to a sandal-thrower and to the obligatory reader of entrails. She was told there was also a woman who read the coffee beans, but that she had been called away elsewhere to attend to a client. "Lucky people," Hawecha thought, "to have so many of us to help them."

The reader of entrails was particularly charming and asked Hawecha if she would read with him. "You are clairvoyant, so it should be easy for you." She promised to be present at the proper time.

When it came, he saw plenty of rain for them all and good health for those present at the ceremony; Hawecha's insight was not quite so reassuring. She foresaw another war, but far into the future, perhaps ten years away.

Hawecha was irate. Were her people to be decimated by others until they vanished off the face of the earth? She complained to several *gadamoji* until she heard from them that the Oromo were not the only people suffering. The Gabbra were also in the midst of tribal clashes as were the Konso, to their west.

The ceremonies began. Hawecha took on the role of teacher again, passing on her knowledge to women, young girls and boys.

All the time, Hawecha was aware of the gnawing pain in her side. Her herbal remedies had done nothing to heal the root cause of her illness which she now knew to be a failing heart. The pain responded only to soporifics and soon she had not enough left. By the end of the ceremonies, she had no strength for the ceremonies of the first-born. She yearned only for peace and quiet and a prolonged rest.

She knew that life was shortening for her, dramatically, and that she needed to find her new home. "Sirius, I am so very tired by now. Please help me find my last hut. Please tell me where it should be!"

The answer came immediately. She was to look for a small village north of the *gadamoji* settlement.

For the last time, she loaded up her donkey and made her way. She proceeded slowly, resting frequently and allowing all to help her.

Bowed and shrunken, she arrived in the village Sirius had indicated. Hawecha had suddenly grown old. They asked what ailed her. "Too much war," she moaned. "All I see is war: behind me, around me and in the years ahead. I cannot teach in times of war. My heart aches too much I need to be quiet now."

They built her a hut, facing north, as she requested. They brought her water daily. A young girl swept for her, whilst another ran her errands. Women cooked for her or invited her to share the evening meal.

Hawecha occasionally felt compelled to teach, since it took her mind off her pain. She found solace in the age-old legends: the First Five Teachers, the Creation and the Flood. Perhaps through their re-telling, she could hold the future at bay. She still told a good story with a beginning, a middle and an end. Whenever she announced that she was going to teach, all the villagers gathered around.

No longer was she just a teacher of women. The men came also and listened.

# CHAPTER 49

"You will come home soon, Hawecha. You are well-prepared." The voice was that of her father and, once more, Hawecha was in mid-sleep. Behind him stood her mother, holding a little girl by the hand. With joy, Hawecha realised it was Dhaki, her own small sister, who had died so long ago.

"I'm waiting for you, Hawecha. How I long to see you again!"

Suleh came to visit in spirit. "What a good life you have led, my dear. Look back, and see how much good you have done, and all that you have accomplished." Obediently, Hawecha reviewed her life, one facet at a time.

She thought of the high priest and all the elders for whom she had caused so much trouble as a young woman. For a time, she had upset time-honoured tradition. She thought of the many whom she had healed, more than making up for her early misdemeanours.

*"Naga! Naga!"* cries of peace echoed in her head. Yes, she had foretold a war and saved several generations from untimely death. Those who had hearkened to her prophecy and had elected to move out of danger had flourished and proliferated. The thought of all the age-sets that in the future would owe their existence to her, filled her with awe. Her successes mounted by the thousands and maybe hundreds and hundreds of thousands. It was only right and fitting that she had earned the title of Prophetess.

She saw the many groups that had at one time or another gathered around her. Several generations had learned the old ways from her. Here too, she must have affected the lives of thousands.

As for her personal triumphs, she had almost fulfilled her childhood dream. She had been to Mega and Tuqqa. Oda had eluded her, but she had made up for it by travelling all the way to Negeleh instead. She had visited Mount Abunu and she had traversed Fugug. The fascinating places she had been to had enriched her life, each in its own way.

The only failure she could recall was in the matter of throwing sandals.

Following these scenes of long ago came other visions and insights, pertaining to the future and the afterlife.

She saw a high priest sitting surrounded by elders. Her own father approached them, to plead her case. The high priest nodded his head sagaciously and announced that Hawecha was welcome. She understood that her father had somehow become a high councillor. Apparently, one could evolve 'up there' too!

Hawecha saw Suleh beckoning to her; there was a group of six or seven small girls who all needed mothering from her. This scene was yet to come. She saw her future-self bend down to hug the littlest one. She knew her. It was the child with the lisp who had brought her water at the 'lawmakers' gathering! Hawecha found her thoughts swinging between past and future. At first she thought she had lost her mind until her visions turned coherent and lucid.

Suleh spoke. "Hawecha, you are an expert on the story of the soul. One day, you will tell people what they did in other lifetimes, and why they have come to earth again. Don't be afraid of this knowledge. People will want to know."

Hawecha found her mind dragged backwards into seemingly ancient history. She saw herself as a young woman, alone and cast out, dying slowly of malnutrition and leprosy. She saw a young man making marks upon hewn stone. She saw a massive stone structure leading up to the clouds and herself inside it teaching a young man some holy words. It all spun around her until she felt sure she was on the point of dying. They were all *her,* those ancient lives, both male and female. Hawecha wondered what dreadful sins she had committed in those lives, that had brought her back into this one.

"Some lives were good and some were not quite so good, Hawecha, "Suleh soothed her. "Three times, you came only to teach; you had such a love for it."

"And now, I can teach no more." Hawecha's soul arose in open rebellion."What is the point of life, if it leads only to death and endings? A teacher should live forever!"

Utterly exhausted by this outburst, she sank back onto her goat skins.

"Those who have finished with earth-life *do* live forever, as I do. You have heard of this before. One day, you will join us. See! Your father calls."

"Death is close, Hawecha. You must thank all those who have helped you."

Hawecha intoned the names .... a long, long list of them: Gababa Halekhe and Dabassah; Suleh and Sirius; Sofmari; her father and mother; Choleh — her childhood friend; Bonsa-The-Midwife; her aunt and uncle; so many helpful hands.

In the morning, Hawecha was surprised to find herself still living. So far away had she been in mind and spirit. She closed her eyes. These thoughts were the harbingers of death. When, oh! When would it come? She prayed for it to come gently, as befitted one who had always fought for peace.

# CHAPTER 50

Three days later, when the girl who swept out her hut came to begin her work, she was surprised to find Hawecha already washed and wearing her newest goat skins. Of late, she had been sluggish and reluctant to step outside. The girl wondered whence came this sudden spurt of energy.

Hawecha announced that she wished to call the villagers together for the last time. "Tell them they have two days before they must come. Tell them that many must come, for it is very important. Tell them it is the last time Hawecha will speak to them."

Overawed, the girl sped away to carry out these peremptory orders.

At the appointed time, the people gathered beneath the sacred tree outside the settlement. Shepherds came and cattle men came and women and children came. Women with babies in their arms and elders and two *gadamoji* came too. Warriors came, laying down their weapons before entering the holy place.

There was an expectant hush in the air. What news would Hawecha bring them? Would it be a prophecy of yet another terrible famine? Or was it war or illness? They had come because they were all deeply afraid.

At last, supported by a forked stick, Hawecha came before them. She stood there, small yet proud, with an air of pain and suffering about her. When she had their complete attention, Hawecha began her story.

"I wish to tell you of a Great Dream I have had." She began. "Do not be afraid, for it is not a terrible one." Her audience relaxed visibly; some sat down upon the ground.

"I saw myself in a strange land, yet I knew it was part of this Earth. I was standing on bright green grass. There were many tall and shady trees, different from this one." She painted a beautiful verbal picture.

"Around me were bushes with bright coloured flowers on them – flowers I have never seen. And in the bushes were many birds. Not like the birds that I know."

They could see that she was tiring and under great strain. Her voice began to tremble. An old woman brought her a stool and urged her to sit. Hawecha acquiesced. For a while, she seemed unable to continue.

She found her voice at last. "The birds spoke to me asking me to come soon, which means that I will die very soon. Birds know these things and I know them too, of course."

The people murmured in consternation. This was not what they had expected. Ignoring them, her voice a little more feeble, Hawecha continued with her dream.

"Then, I saw an amazing thing. Until now, I had only looked around me seeing the grass and bushes and flowers. And the tall trees too, which gave such lovely shade. Now, I looked at myself."

She paused dramatically for maximum effect. After all, she was still a story-teller and had to capture her listeners' hearts. The people sat up, anxious to hear what happened next.

"I was not brown as I am now. My skin was white like milk. Not light brown like the Portuguese invaders of our history. I had become a different kind of person." There was much muttering and commenting at this. Nobody had seen a white person. Perhaps it was a kind of illness?

"I was standing there in front of them all and I was teaching."

Ah, so it was not an illness after all!

"There were many people sitting on the grass around me." Hawecha resumed. "I looked at them all and saw that some were brown like we are and some were very black. Many were white like milk. It was as though all the people of the world had come together. I was teaching them, just as I have taught you. I was talking about the moon, the stars and God. I was exactly the same person. I was laughing happily. It looked like a very nice place to be in. Everyone was so friendly."

Another pause, whilst her audience assimilated these facts. Another lineage? Clearly another country. So, Hawecha would not live on Venus like Suleh did. Hawecha would come back.

And then she stood up with the aid of her stick and all fell silent.

"As I looked carefully at all these people, one by one, I recognised them. Some came into my dream and then left. Never mind what colour their skin was, somehow I knew who they really were. My mother, who died long ago, was there, also in a white skin. A little girl I once knew was there, a very pale colour like a very clean donkey."

She spoke with absolute conviction. She had never lied. They simply had to believe her.

"The last thing I saw is the reason I have called you around me today. It is very important that I tell you this. I looked carefully at all those strange faces and they were not strange at all. I was teaching, remember. I had to know who was listening. I looked into their eyes and saw the truth there. I looked into their eyes . . . and what do you think I saw?"

Everyone was listening avidly.

Hawecha cast her eyes upon the ground now and continued as if in trance. "I recognised everybody in my dream. I recognized all of *you.* That means all of us will meet again in that strange and beautiful place. I don't know when or where. I cannot tell you more." Her voice grew fainter now. "But one thing I know in my heart and in my soul. I will teach you all again. *All* of you were there!"